MAESTRO

Peter Goldsworthy

MAESTRO

HARPER PERENNIAL

Harper*Perennial*
An imprint of HarperCollins*Publishers*

First published in Australia by Angus & Robertson Publishers in 1989
Imprint Classics edition published in 1990
A&R Classics edition published in 2001
This HarperPerennial edition published in 2004
by HarperCollins*Publishers* Australia Pty Limited
ABN 36 009 913 517
A member of the HarperCollins*Publishers* (Australia) Pty Limited Group
www.harpercollins.com.au

Copyright © Peter Goldsworthy 1989

HarperCollins*Publishers*
25 Ryde Road, Pymble, Sydney, NSW 2073, Australia
31 View Road, Glenfield, Auckland 10, New Zealand
77–85 Fulham Palace Road, London W6 8JB, United Kingdom
2 Bloor Street East, 20th floor, Toronto, Ontario M4W 1A8, Canada
10 East 53rd Street, New York NY 10022, USA

National Library of Australia Cataloguing-in-Publication data:

Goldsworthy, Peter, 1951– .
  Maestro.
  ISBN 0 7322 8148 2.
  1. Pianist – Fiction. 2. Holocaust survivors – Australia – Fiction.
  3. Darwin (N.T.) – Fiction. I. Title.
A823.3

Cover design by Mary Callahan
Cover image by Getty Images
Printed and bound in Australia by Griffin Press on 50gsm Bulky News

5 4   06 07 08

To four pianists: my parents Jan and Reuben,
my daughter Anna, and the finest teacher I have known,
Eleanora Sivan

Acknowledgments

The author would like to thank Philippe Tanguy for his tireless and creative editing. He would also like to thank Brisbane Grammar School for providing a period as writer-in-residence which enabled him to begin this book, and the South Australian Government through the Department for the Arts for the grant which provided time to complete it.

Versions of several chapters first appeared in the *Sydney Review*, the *Adelaide Review*, and the *Sydney Morning Herald Literary Supplement*.

The poem quoted in the final chapter is a version of *Wo*? by Heinrich Heine, rendered into approximate English by the author.

Through her political scandals Austria has managed to draw the big world's attention to herself—and at last is no longer confused with Australia.

Karl Kraus

Contents

Darwin, 1967	1
Intermezzo	51
1968	61
Adelaide	93
1974	121
Vienna, 1975	129
1977	141

Darwin, 1967

*F*irst impressions?

Misleading, of course. As always. But unforgettable: the red glow of his face—a boozer's incandescent glow. The pitted, sun-coarsened skin—a cheap, ruined leather. And the eyes: an old man's moist, wobbling jellies.

But then . . . the suit: white linen, freshly pressed. And—absurdly, in that climate—the stiff collar and tie.

'Herr Keller?'

'Mrs Crabbe?'

I stood behind my mother outside his room at the *Swan*, perched on a wooden balcony overlooking the beer garden. The hotel—a warren of crumbling weatherboard, overgrown with bougainvillea—was packed, the drinkers and their noise spilling out of the front bar into the garden. Up the stairs, second on the right, a barman had shouted—and every face in the bar had turned and followed us up. One or two drunken whistles had also followed us up; whistles living far beyond their sexual means, my mother later reported to my father, contemptuously.

'This is Paul,' she said, pushing me forward, ignoring the noise below.

The figure in the white suit stood aside from his doorway, and motioned us inside.

'Of course. Your father has told.'

The accent was thick. Continental, my father had described it, vaguely. A voice that reminded him of grilling sausages: a faint, constant spitting of sibilants in the background.

'Sit down,' the voice hissed. 'We will talk.'

A problem: how to capture that accent here? *Ve vill talk?* It's tempting—too tempting—to slip into comic-book parody. *We haf ways off makink . . .*

If I were less the musician and more the dramatist perhaps I could capture it. No: if I were *more* the musician, if I had a better ear, I could surely capture it—invent some new notation to pin those strange melodies to the page. But that looks too much like hard work. And might prove too distracting. What matters is the content: *what* he said, not how.

So, a declaration: from this point in my memoir Keller—Herr Eduard Keller, the maestro—will speak English as well, or as badly, as me.

The room behind his door above the beer garden was large, but somehow shrunken, diminished by the presence of the two pianos. An upright, and (my father's favourite joke) a supine. Those pianos filled the available space like two planets, or perhaps a planet and its smaller moon; about them all else revolved. It took some effort to notice the other furnishings on that first visit: the narrow bed jammed against one wall, the shelves crammed floor-to-ceiling with books and sheet music, the washbasin, the single armchair.

Keller led my mother to the armchair and seated her with a formal, mannered courtliness; ridiculous, yes, but somehow natural at the same time. In retrospect I seem to hear the click of heels coming together, distinctly—but this surely was not so.

He seated himself at the grand—a *Bösendorfer*, the first I'd seen—and swivelled to face us. The upright—a peeling *Wertheim*, its varnish cracked and bubbled by too many years too near the equator—was mine.

He pointed at the stool. I sat.

For a time he said nothing, watching. His red face glowed above the white collar and lapels. Some internal explosion seemed to have driven a thousand broken blood vessels against the inside of his cheeks. Outside, the sound of thunder carried to us, distantly: the sound of February, of deepest, darkest Wet. The room was stifling, oppressive, but the louvred wooden slats that formed two opposing walls remained closed, the ceiling fan stilled. Not a whisper of movement stirred in the sticky air.

I sensed that I was undergoing some form of test.

'Heat,' Keller suddenly pronounced, 'we can withstand. A little discomfort is necessary to maintain alertness. But noise . . .'

He gestured in the direction of the louvred wall that faced onto the balcony—the direction of the beer garden below.

My mother smiled uncertainly and dabbed a handkerchief at her brow. The sweat was beginning to gather, the droplets aggregating into larger drops, heavy as mercury. Newcomers in Darwin, we had moved from the temperate South barely a month before: she found the climate unbearable.

Keller's red face also glistened with a fine varnish of sweat— but the linen suit still seemed crisp and freshly laundered. Had he spruced up especially to meet me? I was child enough— self-centred enough—to think it likely..

He stared; I stared boldly back, fascinated. I'd seen nothing like him before. He was short: migrant-height, European-height. Wop-height. The hair above that flaming face was white, sparse, downy. On his red nose he had placed what I somehow instantly recognised as a pince-nez—although I had come across only the word before, in books, never the actual thing.

Above all, I remember the hands: those dainty, faintly ridiculous hands.

I couldn't take my eyes away from them. Small and podgy like inflated gloves, they narrowed delicately, fastidiously, towards the tips of the fingers. The nails were manicured; the skin pale and soft and clean. If his face was coarse leather, his hands were fashioned from the finest calf: each wrinkle, each dimple carefully hand-tooled.

A pianist's hands? Impossible. Too unfunctional, surely. Too . . . decorative. Incapable of straddling a fifth, let alone an octave.

One other thing: most of the right little finger was missing. A gold ring on the stump seemed to deliberately flaunt its absence.

'Fifth fingers are unnecessary,' he pronounced, suddenly.

I squirmed, disconcerted, and looked in another direction.

'I wasn't . . . I mean, I didn't mean . . .'

'A luxury,' he continued. 'No pianist before Chopin used the fifth finger.'

He told me this so often in the following years that I soon realised the loss meant far more to him than that.

'Mozart never used the little fingers,' he continued, waggling the stump. 'Old Bach. Clementi.'

5

'And after Chopin?' I found my tongue again.

'Excuse?'

'Can you play Liszt without it?' I spoke up, ignoring my mother's warning glance.

He answered this as he was often to answer, by turning abruptly to the keyboard. And here a miracle occurred: the first of many miracles, or sleights of hand, that I was to witness in his presence. Somehow that tiny, maimed claw released an effortless, rippling run of tenths.

'The little finger is a lazy fellow,' he smiled, lifting the hand from the keyboard and waggling the stump once more in my face. 'He can be trained, yes. Perhaps we will train yours. But he can be done without.'

He reached over and seized my little fingers—one in each hand.

'If we tell him he can be done without, perhaps he will try harder.'

A joke? It was becoming more and more difficult to tell. My mother managed to produce an amused sort of noise.

'How old are these hands?' he asked, still grasping my fingers, turning them this way and that.

'Pardon?' I said.

'These hands—how old?'

'Paul is fifteen,' my mother interposed.

'Large hands,' he said. 'Difficult to control. But we have time.'

'Shall I play something?' I suggested.

He smiled at me for the first time: a brief, minimal smile.

'No,' he said. 'I have heard hands like this before. I know how they sound.'

I glanced at my mother for help, but she avoided my eyes.

'Today we will only look,' he continued. 'At hands. And fingers.'

He immediately began to explain, in language I thought simple and patronising, that five very different personalities were attached to the human hand.

'They are great friends. A circle of friends. But also great rivals.'

His thumb ground painfully into the flesh of my upper arm. I bit my lip, trying not to cry out. I could sense my mother shift in her chair, startled.

'Thumb is . . . too strong. A rooster, a show-off. Sultan of the harem. He must be kept in place.'

He leant back, amused, watching me rub at the bruise on my arm.

'But perhaps that is enough for this week. Next week . . . the forefinger.'

'Then you will take him?' my mother asked.

'We will see.'

*A*t home, my mother dabbed at her brow with a wet flannel she kept in the fridge for that purpose.

'I hereby grant permission,' she murmured, flushed, smiling, 'for you to attend all future piano lessons alone.'

She cranked open the wall louvres to maximum aperture, returned the wet flannel to the fridge, and decanted two iced lemon drinks. For some time we sat sipping in silence, the only sounds those of the ice-cubes chinking in their glasses and the ceiling fan whirring at highest notch above us.

We were still sipping our drinks when car tyres crunched across the gravel drive and into the shelter beneath us. As always my mother rose at the sound and began fussing in the kitchen—pulling dishes from the fridge, tossing salads.

'Well?' my father asked, entering.

The question was directed at me.

'It went OK.'

He set down his briefcase and began riffling through the mail on the sideboard—to see if his knighthood had arrived, he liked to joke.

'Did he like your playing?'

'I didn't play.'

At this he glanced up: 'You didn't *play*?'

'Herr Keller said he knew how it would sound,' my mother

called across the narrow workbench that separated kitchen from lounge. 'Quote, unquote.'

'Without listening?'

'He's an original,' she laughed. 'White suit. Pith helmet.'

'*Pith* helmet?'

'Perhaps I made that part up. But I like him.'

'*I* don't,' I muttered. 'He practically broke my arm.'

I had been stewing over the events of that lesson ever since we'd left the *Swan*.

'I'm serious. He's a sadist. He . . .'

'That's enough,' my father ordered, quietly.

I sat nursing my drink, cooling both hands on the damp, dewy glass. In the same manner I had many times, in the South, warmed *cold* hands, on *hot* drinks. My father remained silent.

'Why can't I learn from *you*?' I said, at length.

'Must we go through this again?' he answered. 'You are going to be better than me. *Much* better.'

And that's an order, I whispered to myself, soundlessly.

'Perhaps there is some other teacher in Darwin,' my mother, ever the conciliator, suggested.

He snorted: 'There's no-one. It's a town of drunks.'

He had not had a good day, it seemed. Again.

'All the scum in the country has somehow risen to this one town,' he declared, as he had been declaring, daily, since our arrival. 'All the drifters, the misfits. The wife-bashers . . .'

'You *wanted* to come,' she chided him gently. 'You agreed to the transfer.'

'I agreed to the *promotion*.'

'He's not sure,' I intervened, 'if he wants me.'

'He's teasing you,' my father said. 'He's had no-one as good as you before. Besides, he needs the money.'

He winked at my mother, and tilted an imaginary glass towards his mouth, thinking perhaps that I wouldn't understand.

'I'm told he has expensive habits.'

'His physiognomy,' she murmured, 'would lend support to that hypothesis.'

Often they chose to speak in this enigmatic manner: a private code of polysyllables for Adults Only information, a code I had long broken.

'A dipsomaniac?' my father continued speaking in code, perhaps for the fun of it.

'A weakness for bibacity.'

'You mean he's a boozer?' I decided to spoil the fun.

After dinner that night the two of them played a duet: Mozart, always his preferred tranquilliser when irritable. At first I kept my distance, sitting on the far side of the room, still angry. But the music, as always, drew me—that beautiful, tugging gravity—and soon I was standing at their side, flipping the pages of the score, watching their fingers flickering across the keys.

Watching especially their *fifth* fingers—all four fifth fingers—flickering across the keys. I didn't believe a word Keller had said.

During the slow movement the rain began again. It fell abruptly, totally, a solid volume of water descending on the iron roof. The two of them kept playing—two parts, now, of a mismatched Trio—but after a few bars they abandoned the attempt, leaving the rain, deafening, solo.

My father loosened his tie. In those first weeks he still clung to the Southerner's uniform. Then he wiped the sweat from his brow.

'The arsehole of the earth,' he declared, loudly.

He dropped the piano lid with a thud.

'A city of booze, blow, and blasphemy,' he said, in the tone of voice he reserved for memorable quotes.

'Shakespeare?' my mother wondered.

He shook his head: 'Banjo Paterson.'

I loved the town of booze and blow at first sight. And above all its *smell*: those hot, steamy perfumes that wrapped about me as we stepped off the plane, in the darkness, in the smallest hours of a January night. Moist, compost air. Sweet-and-sour air . . .

We spent the remaining few hours of that first night in

a motel room, but I couldn't sleep. Sometime near dawn I jerked the mosquito netting aside, rose from the bed and peered out through the louvres. Always I'll remember that first morning: the brilliant furnace of the rising sun; the huge clouds that ruddered the sky. In every direction rain could be seen falling: vast, distant cubes of water dropping slowly, ponderously out of the sky.

From time to time a cube would descend from directly above: not so much rain as a solid mass of water, beginning and ceasing suddenly.

Mid-morning found us inspecting our new home: a bare shoebox of louvred walls and asbestos, perched above the wet shrubbery on high, thin stork-stilts.

'Is this it?' My mother tried to disbelieve.

'This is it.'

'Check the number again . . .'

'This is it,' my father repeated.

'Perhaps the key won't fit,' she hoped.

Later that morning I found her sitting on the edge of the bath, weeping silently: she had left a bluestone villa in the South for this.

Later still—rubber-gloved, aproned, her thick hair stuffed beneath a scarf, some sort of personal crisis reached and passed—she began preparing the house for the arrival of the furniture.

I spent most of that first day outside, ducking back beneath the house during downpours. I was keeping out of range of the unpacking, yes—out of sight, out of mind—but also exploring. The garden was large and wet and green, growing dense with trees and shrubbery at the back where it merged without obvious boundaries into a jungled gully which led down to the mangroves and tidal flats.

I clambered eagerly down among the slippery shrubs, slipping and sliding through the dense undergrowth. I had never seen such greenness: an unnatural greenness, as if the leaves were a kind of plastic. Huge parrots yattered in the dripping fruit trees. Butterflies of brilliant colours—bright rainbow colours, chemistry set colours, coffee-table book colours—filled the air. Under any leaf I chose to lift small creatures seemed hidden: giant, clockwork insects, built from strange meccano, or grubs the size of small, juicy mammals.

Cartoon descriptions? How else to describe a cartoon world? The moths that thudded into the flyscreens that night were the size of bats—soft, powdery bats. And the bats that filled the mango trees in the darkening twilight were foxes. Even our garden lawn—most domesticated of foliage—needed mowing again almost as soon as it was done . . . like some lush, green five o'clock shadow.

Everything grew larger than life in the steamy hothouse of Darwin, and the people were no exception.

Exotic, hothouse blooms.

———— ◆ ————

Keller waggled a forefinger in front of my nose. It was our second lesson? Our third?

'This finger is selfish. Greedy. A . . . a delinquent. He will steal from his four friends, cheat, lie.'

He sheathed the forefinger in his closed fist as if it were the fleshy blade of a Swiss army knife and released the middle finger.

'Mr goody-goody,' he said, banging the finger down on middle C repeatedly. 'Teacher's pet. Does what he is told. Our best student.'

Last came the ring finger.

'Likes to follow his best friend,' he told me. 'Likes to . . . lean on him sometimes.'

He lifted his elbows upwards and outwards.

'Those are the pupils. This is the teacher. The elbow . . .'

I noticed that his elbows—the elbows of that pressed white suit—were always smudged with grime. In the months to come—as I rode past the *Swan* to school each morning— I would often pass him, seated at a table on his balcony, sipping coffee, leaning his elbows on a pile of newspapers.

It became a game for me during the lessons, during the endless drill of scales and arpeggios, to try to decipher the smudged headlines, reversed, on the elbows and sleeves of his coat. SHOCK, I imagined I could make out from time to time. HORROR. PROBE. Plus, once, clearly: *DIE ZEIT*, the words this time not only reversed but foreign.

'. . . and this,' he continued, tapping me on the forehead, 'is the headmaster. Now, you and your ten pupils may play for me.'

'Chopin?'

He grimaced. 'If you must.'

I was incredulous: 'You don't like Chopin?'

'On the contrary. I like Chopin very much. That is the point.'

I said nothing, infuriated. I, too, would let my hands do the talking. I dropped them to the keyboard.

But before a single note had been played he reached over and seized my wrists.

'No,' he said. 'No more. I do not like your Chopin.'

'But I haven't started!'

'You *have* of course started. Your hands are in the wrong position. Also your fingertips. Your elbows. I do not have to listen. I know how your Chopin would sound.'

'My mother said it was excellent.'

'Your mother is a fine woman, but she does not fully understand Chopin. Fortunately—unlike you—she understands that she does not understand.'

He was still squeezing my wrists. I struggled to free them, but his grip was too strong.

'I want to play!' I blurted out. 'My parents are paying you to teach me to play.'

'You are spoilt,' he said. 'First you must learn to listen.'

He released me, plucked my copy of the *Nocturnes* from the piano, and shook his head sadly.

'Also,' he said. 'This edition . . . a joke. Unplayable.'

He dropped the book into a wastebin at his feet.

The injustice of it all overwhelmed me. Tears seeped from my eyes, a lump clogged my throat.

'I want to go home,' I said.

'You are free to leave my home,' he answered. 'At any time. But you are *not* free to play in my home without my permission.'

I retrieved my *Nocturnes* from the bin and ran from his room, ran down the stairs past the beer garden in full bloom below, through the front bar crowded with those who believed Bach was the noise that cattle dogs made, and Chopin the function of an axe, and pushed out into the street, vowing never to return, weeping tears of rage.

———— ◆ ————

*S*itting here, setting down these first memories of Keller— and checking them through, believing them accurate— I find it hard to understand how much I came to love the man, to depend on him. At the time (and again now, reliving that time) it seemed—*seems*—impossible.

'I'm not going to any more lessons,' I announced over dinner.

'You will do as you are told,' my father said.

'He won't even let me *play*.'

'We must give him time,' my mother bargained.

'He's a Nazi.'

Without warning, my father reached across and seized me violently by the shirt-front. Buttons popped. A wineglass cartwheeled across the table.

'Go,' he said, but quietly, already regretting the violence, 'to your room.'

My mother came gently knocking on my door a little later. I slid the comic I was reading into a drawer of my desk and reached for *Intermediate Latin*.

'Your father's been under a lot of pressure,' she said. 'At the hospital. And the climate doesn't help.'

She stood behind me, resting her hands on my shoulders. The sound of Mozart began to flow from the front room: K. 283, the *Adagio*, a tranquil river.

'Do you understand why he was so angry?'

I leant back into her: 'Swearing?'

13

'No,' she said. 'Not swearing. It was because you called Herr Keller a Nazi.'

'If the jackboot fits . . .'

I could sense her shaking her head, the movement transmitted, faintly, through her chest pressed against me. I knew she was smiling, despite herself.

'You know so much for your age,' she said. 'And so little.'

She often spoke in riddles when things got serious.

'It's important to your father,' she said, 'that you continue the lessons.'

This was another of her speech habits when things got serious. Your Father. Never My Husband. Or Dad. Or John.

'Your Father,' I murmured, inaudibly. 'Which Art . . .'

'Your Father never had your opportunities,' she continued, the words still upper-case and reverential. 'He always regretted it. You must understand: we lost so much time in the War. And after the War there was no time for music. If he seems hard on you, it's because of that.'

'But why Keller?'

'Must we go through this again?'

'If Dad is so impressed with Keller let *him* learn from him.'

She paused before continuing, as if making some sort of decision.

'He asked,' she finally admitted. 'Keller said he was too old. Fixed habits.'

As always, my father checked my room after Lights Out. I feigned sleep, but felt the approaching footsteps, the floor vibrating gently beneath my bed, and the quick kiss on the temple . . .

And heard the squeak of the louvred walls opening, and the sudden thunder of the frogs down in the gully outside—a choir of a million voices, revelling after the latest deluge. Filling the room, deafeningly.

To describe the world is always to simplify its texture, to coarsen the weave: to lose the particular in the general. But as I sit here writing, the events of my childhood seem to fall naturally into patterns, to *want* to fit themselves into simple, easily remembered categories. The past forms up into neat lines, assembles itself as if in a school quadrangle, or in a child's exercise book, under the simplest of headings: *My First Piano Lesson. Our House In Darwin. What I Did During The Holidays. My Parents* . . .

But perhaps this last heading should be teased apart, split in two: *Mum, and Dad. Nancy, and John.*

Apart from the piano they had little in common. When I think of my parents I see only polarities. Hard, and soft. Fair, and dark. Thin, and thick.

They might have belonged to different species. Which would make me . . . what? Some sort of mule?

The list of their differences is inexhaustible. Tall, and short. Stoic, emotional. Quiet, talkative. Does it matter which was which? Perhaps not, but in those pairing of opposites I have always put my father first.

They disagreed on everything—but frivolously, teasingly. It was a kind of game, played endlessly throughout my childhood: a choosing up of sides.

'The Haydn?' from my short, dark mother.

'*I* would prefer the Mozart,' from my tall, fair father.

'The D flat major?'

'The G minor.'

'The Allegro?'

'The Adagio.'

And so on through Bach and Handel; Schubert, Schumann; Chopin, Liszt—their opinions as black and white as the notes on any keyboard. Beyond the world of music this gentle war continued; favourite colours: blue, green; favourite cities: Sydney, Melbourne; even, once, I remember, favourite Big *Cats*!

'Tigers,' my mother tugged gently at one hand as we entered the wrought iron gates of the Adelaide Zoo, 'This way.'

'Lions,' my father tugged more firmly at the other, '*Real* cats over here.'

No issue was too trivial to prevent some half-teasing, half-serious disagreement. I remember once reading of a lost valley where the men and women spoke a different tongue. My parents might have belonged to that tribe. The two languages they spoke sounded the same, but the words held different meanings. Take the most ordinary noun, *any* ordinary noun: 'dog', for instance. To my mother it meant licks and games and companionship. To my father it meant cleaning shit off his shoes. Even their senses of time were different—as if they lived in different time zones, at different longitudes. 'Noon' to my mother was a vague, elastic region located somewhere between breakfast and dusk. To my father it was 12 sharp, Central Standard Time—give or take a handful of seconds, depending on mood.

I could list their entire separate vocabularies like this: every meaning completely opposed. And yet how happy they always seemed, in spite, or perhaps *because* of it. Something bound them together—some deeper language held in common. The sweet, sticky glue of sex perhaps . . .

But that is guesswork. I was still a child then, innocent of things sweet and sticky. At night their bedroom door was always closed.

Music was another glue. To both my parents, music was their true career. There was never much money in the house: my father was always more interested in making music than money. He practised medicine more as an intellectual hobby than as a livelihood. A Government Medical Officer, the effort of setting up a private practice seemed beyond him. My mother likewise: a librarian before marriage, she had preferred the role of Housewife and Mother since; but worked only part-time at *that*, spending less time each day on housework than sitting at the piano.

Yet even here there was an enormous gulf between them. To my father, music was a species of time: the piano was an interesting kind of clock mechanism—a *measuring* instrument. My mother was sloppier, allowing herself more mistakes, but in the end she had more fun. Duke Ellington would stroll down the keyboard between Debussy and Schumann. A Beethoven sonata might be interrupted, mid-allegro, by *I'm Getting Married in the Morning*.

All of which left me—their crossbreed, their mulatto—where? One thing is certain: I grew up in a sense bilingually, always able to see both sides of an argument.

Which is, as my father often told me, a polite way of saying I'm unable to make up my mind.

That I'm a fence-sitter.

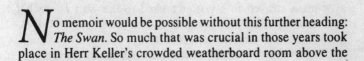

No memoir would be possible without this further heading: *The Swan*. So much that was crucial in those years took place in Herr Keller's crowded weatherboard room above the front bar of the *Swan*.

Outside in Darwin the rains came and went, but it was always Wet season in the front bar of the *Swan*: a monsoon of beer and sweat and smoke and noise. I pushed through the storm each Tuesday on my way to piano lessons, and out again afterwards. Overhead the big fans turned—slowly, slowly—stirring it all into one thick, exhausted atmosphere, seemingly unbreathable, uninhabitable . . .

And yet its inhabitants somehow survived. And only grew noisier, and thirstier, the longer they stayed. In the muggy heat of the evening the chinking of cold glasses drew them from every corner of the town, like tiny glass bells tolling for Mass, tolling for a communion of beer and tobacco.

A Mass taken in remembrance of nothing more than the previous night's beer and tobacco.

They sought forgetfulness, not remembrance. Who could blame them? Over dinner each night, my father recounted the day's horror stories from his work at the hospital. He spared us nothing; stories of wife-beaters, fugitives from justice, alcoholics and maintenance dodgers. Darwin was the terminus, he liked to say: the Top End of the road. A town populated by men who had run as far as they could flee. From here there was only one further escape. And each day on his rounds he saw any number of those hell bent on taking it.

As I pushed my way through the drinkers each Tuesday, clutching my music satchel, I found it easy to place Keller among these fugitives.

17

A Nazi, I had called him after that first piano lesson, using the word then in some loose generic sense—but more and more now I really began to wonder. The word stuck in my mind—a particle of impurity around which further pieces of evidence began wrapping themselves . . . a crystal of suspicion, growing in layers . . .

As he talked or played his way through the lessons my eyes often strayed to a poster tacked to the wall above his bed: an idyllic European scene of church spires, stone bridges, pool-blue river—and the letters WIEN.

I knew almost nothing about him. Austrian, German . . . what was the difference?

I had read my share of war comics, and was reading them still. I had even read my share of headlines: Adolf Eichmann, kidnapped not so long ago from South America and hanged for war crimes in Israel, had been Austrian, I knew. *Adolf Hitler* had been Austrian . . .

And so lying in bed at night, tossing sleeplessly beneath the overhead fan, rewinding and replaying to myself each Tuesday afternoon's humiliations, I became determined to expose Eduard Keller as the War Criminal I suspected he was . . .

Eduard Keller? It was *Adolf* Keller, surely—or so I found it amusing to think of him.

—— ◆ ——

*P*layed anything yet?'

My father's weekly joke was uttered over dinner every Tuesday evening, after my latest 'consultation' with Adolf.

'Nothing yet.'

'A quaver?'

I isolated a single pea on my plate and sliced it carefully, absurdly in half, and then into quarters, irritated by his questions.

'A *semi*quaver?' my mother added, joining in the joking, perhaps even sending herself up, her own usual role of mediator.

'I'm not allowed to play for another month. Not even scales.'

'Surely you can practise at home.'

'*Especially* not at home, unsupervised. He wants me to forget everything I've been taught.'

My mother worried: 'You don't think that's going a little too far, John?'

He snorted. 'Farmers are paid not to grow crops. We pay Keller to stop Paul making music. Possibly it will increase the value of the product.'

My mother decided to change the subject. 'What do you do?' she asked, 'during these . . . consultations?'

'We talk,' I said. 'No: *he* talks. I listen.'

'What did you talk about today?' She tried to be interested.

'The lengths of fingers.'

'I'm sorry?'

'He explained that the fingers on our hands are not all the same length.'

Concerned glances were exchanged between my parents.

I held up my hand, and mimicked, falsetto: 'Ze middle finger is longer zan ze forefinger. Ze forefinger . . .'

'Very profound.' My father shook his head, bemused. His initial enthusiasm for Keller was beginning to wane.

'There's more,' I said. 'He then told me that the keys on a piano *are* all the same length.'

They sat holding their knives and forks above their food, becalmed by curiosity.

'Is there a moral in this?' my mother eventually asked.

'He asked me what we could do to remedy this . . . mismatching.'

'Even up our fingers with a hacksaw?' my father suggested.

I laughed, wishing I had used the same answer. Then—remembering Keller's stumpy little finger—I was glad that I hadn't.

'He also talked about his ancestors.'

'His family?'

'His *musical* ancestors.'

'Tell us,' my mother urged.

'Beethoven begat Czerny,' I recited as best I could. 'Czerny begat Liszt. Liszt begat Lecherovsky—or someone. And Lecherovsky begat . . . Keller.'

My father's fork again halted mid-air.

'His teacher learnt from *Liszt*?'

'Apparently.' I shrugged my shoulders.

'Impossible.' My father shook his head. 'He must be pulling your leg.'

My mother rose from the table and tugged the music dictionary, a much-bruised and battered tome, from a nearby bookshelf.

'Liszt died in . . . 1886,' she found, flipping rapidly through. 'What did you say was the name of his teacher?'

'Liszt was taught by Czerny.'

'No—Herr *Keller's* teacher.'

'Lecher something.'

'Leschetizky?'

'Sounds right.'

She flipped back a few pages.

'Leschetizky. Theodore. 1830–1915 . . . um . . . Professor of pianoforte, St Petersburg Conservatorium, 1852–78. Later settled in Vienna where he established his own school.'

'1915.' My father pursed his lips. 'It's possible.'

'He has a poster of Vienna.' I volunteered. 'Stuck on the wall.'

'Among his pupils,' my mother was reading on. 'Paderewski . . . Annette Essipoff.'

Here she paused, then murmured: 'Good Lord!'

'Let me see.' My father reached for the book, but she retained a firm grip with both hands and read on:

'Schnabel . . . Gabrilowitsch . . . Eduard Keller.'

A kind of suppressed excitement filled them: they clutched at the dictionary together, shoulders pressing. My father finally rose from the table, and began pacing restlessly.

'Must be a common name, Keller' he said. 'The Smiths of Austria.'

He paced a little more, not fully convincing himself: 'What on earth would a man like that be doing in *this* place?'

Finding no separate entry under Keller, my mother began

plucking other thick books from the nearby shelves—*Great Pianists, My Life in Music, Lives of the Virtuosi*—searching for clues. Indexes were scrutinised, fruitlessly. Eventually even the record jackets were being pulled from the gramophone cabinet and inspected: the precious Schnabel 78s, the single scratched Paderewski . . . Then my father:

'I'd heard he was a good teacher. No wonder they call him the maestro. I'd always thought it was a joke. Something to do with his temperament.'

'It might not be the same man,' my mother reminded him, her own excitement waning a little as if in counterweight to his. 'Leschetizky probably had any number of students called Keller.'

But my father wanted to believe.

'*Eduard* Keller?' he said. 'The coincidence is too great.'

There was no Mozart after tea that night. Instead my father rummaged in the piano stool for some time, emerging finally with a wodge of torn, yellowing scraps of sheet music which he jigsawed together on the tabletop, bandaging the fissures with sticky tape.

LISZT, I read on the tattered title-page. TRANSCENDENTAL STUDIES.

As I left the room, homework-bound, he was already picking his way slowly through the first bars. At midnight, as I lay in bed, thumbing through my war comics, I could still hear him, faster now, more certain, banging at the keyboard—if not with transcendence, at least with fervour.

'I think I'll come to your next lesson,' he announced in the morning, over breakfast. 'I want to know more about this Eduard Keller.'

Outside the rains were still falling, the air thick and steamy. But from that morning his mood seemed altered, lifted into some zone of clearer, fresher mental weather.

This was not just my imagination: soon there was concrete evidence. His collar and tie vanished on the following Thursday; and on the Friday, after a late-afternoon shopping safari, he adopted local costume completely: shorts, open-necked shirt. Phrases such as *We Territorians* would shortly begin flecking his conversation, especially conversation with visiting Southerners. *In the Top End we do it this way* . . .

He sat in on the next lesson. And the next, clutching his notebook in a corner, jotting down every snippet of advice, every muttered aside, every wandering reverie that Keller produced.

As for the maestro, I doubt he noticed. The lessons continued unchanged: in his own world, in his own time. The prescribed hour might contract into half an hour, or stretch into three— depending on what he wanted to get off his chest.

'When do we finish?' I would ask.

'When I am emptied.'

Also, I suspected, when he was thirsty. As my father and I descended the stairs from his room afterwards, he would often be following close on our heels, heading for the beer garden below.

——— ◆ ———

With the beginning of the school term I began riding my pushbike to school. The shortest route led past the *Swan*, behind the beer garden. I would often pass my former War Criminal, seated at a small table on his balcony, his white Panama somehow remaining stuck to his bent head as he sipped coffee and schnapps and smudged the elbows of his white coat on the morning headlines.

The Southern papers were always days old, and *DIE ZEIT* at least a month. But the Wet season humidity somehow rendered their newsprint moist, as if straight off the press— and this seemed to render the news itself somehow fresher, as if the world were closer than it was.

A pair of scissors and scrapbook were always at his side when he read: from time to time he would snip out some odd geometry of newsprint, a square or oblong or thick T or L, and slip it between the pages of the book.

I always pedalled quickly, smoothly by. If he caught me glancing up, I might acknowledge his wave curtly: a minimal response, the flick of a finger, the tug of an earlobe, as if bidding at some discreet auction . . .

If a friend was cycling with me I ignored his greeting altogether, riding head-down, engrossing myself in a discussion of last night's homework, or Saturday's football.

The friend in those first weeks of school was Bennie Reid, another new arrival in town—in his case from England.

'Look at that pisspot,' Bennie would say, trying out the local slang, pointing to Keller. 'Already into the turps.'

'Where?'

'Up there, in the white hat and bowls outfit. Look—he's waving. You know him?'

We had met, Bennie and I, on the first day of school: marooned alongside each other in a sea of hostile stares. In memory Bennie always remains middle-aged—paunchy, puffy-faced, balding—although I knew him only as an adolescent, and he could not have been balding at fifteen. Oddly accented, gentle, fussy, bespectacled—a violinist, and collector of butterflies—like me he learnt quickly to ride his bike to school rather than risk the terrors of the school-bus.

'That's my seat, Four Eyes. Move.'

'Hey, Four Eyes. Lend me a dollar.'

'Why don't you leave him alone?'

'Fine. *You* lend me the dollar, Big Mouth!'

If I left early enough I could beat both Four Eyes and the bus to school. If I were late he would catch me coasting down Mindil Beach Road, his body shape—more spherical, perhaps, with a higher specific gravity—carrying him further and faster. Then the bus would catch both of us as we crawled in low gear up Bullocky Point, and a monsoon of sandwiches and fruit would rain down from every window.

'Yaah, Four Eyes!'

'Be waiting for you in the bike shed, Big Mouth!'

I soon learnt to avoid the bike shed and the schoolyard as much as possible, to maintain the most minimal profile.

The designated Music Room—a second-floor classroom containing an ageing piano—became my refuge. It seemed safest to practise there each lunchtime, and again after school until the bike shed was clear. If I became tired of practising, there was always the view from the window: the white sands and shallow breaking waves that stretched away like ruled, parallel chalk lines each side of the point.

The High School, isolated on its headland like some kind of quarantine station, or detention centre, seemed miles from the nearest human habitation—but it was probably no more than half a mile.

It *was* three hundred miles from the next school.

And two thousand miles from the nearest university: an immense advantage, some might argue.

At first glance it might have been any Southern school: glass boxes squatting in a sea of asphalt, form matched to function. The one concession to latitude was a vast, covered playing area—protection against the tropical rains. On overcast days during the deep Wet, that roofed area entered a kind of steamy twilight. In its dimly lit corners anything became possible. Patterns of experimental behaviour were pioneered that later became widespread: knife-fights, drunkenness, unspeakable acts beneath ping-pong tables. Small beer now, perhaps, accepted as part of the school curriculum everywhere, but at the cutting edge then. State of the Art delinquency . . .

A thousand students climbed to Bullocky Point by foot, bus, or bike each morning: seven packed First Year classes, seven Second Year classes, and seven Third Year classes—the last year of compulsory education.

There were also two small Fourth Year classes.

And one tiny Matriculation class.

This pyramid of statistics offered no comfort to my parents. The Schooling Debate had begun six months before, while still in the South, with news of my father's posting. It raged well into the first term.

Should I be kept South, in a Good School? All possible pro and con arguments were rostered between the two of them: the first to speak usually proposing the idea, knowing that there was no risk of reaching agreement, relying on the certainty that the other would veto it.

Of course they wanted their only son to remain near for a few years longer. If my mother—say—began to vacillate, to agree with my father that yes, perhaps there *was* merit in sending me South to board, then he also could be relied on to change his mind, and cross the floor in the other direction the moment she was crossing to *his* side.

Which was fine with me. I had no desire for boarding school, a world I had begun to imagine all too well with the help of various English weekly comics that Bennie Reid subscribed to. Ruthless Latin Masters, muddy Rugger Fifteens, and chaps with names like craters in the moon—Spofforth Minor, Bromwich Major—filled those pages.

I preferred Darwin High, if not immediately.

Skinny, unathletic, irredeemably smug, my pen slamming loudly onto my desk at the end of each maths problem to let the plodders know I had finished, the place could—*should*—have been hell on earth. And was, for much of my first year, even if I hid myself whenever possible in the Music Room, and shunned any public association with Bennie Reid.

Weekends this was not so easy. Our parents, church-going acquaintances, often forced us together, concerned about our isolation.

'He's such a nice boy,' my mother gently nagged. 'And he plays the violin.'

'He does *something* to the violin. But I don't think it could be described as playing.'

Away from the rigid schoolyard hierarchy, I was happy enough in Bennie's company—or not unhappy. I refused to play duets with him, to accompany his inept fiddle-scrapings, but often found myself wandering in his wake through some mangrove swamp or tract of bush, spare butterfly net in hand.

Briefly, episodically, his enthusiasm infected me. A constant flickering confetti of butterflies showered the town of Darwin. Designer insects, I think of them now: there was something enormously wasteful, extravagant even, about the profusion of patterns and shapes and brilliant colours. What point such an oversupply of beauty, except for the pleasure of collectors such as Bennie?

Hunting, he was transformed: no bush was too thorny, no tree too tall, no cliff edge too sheer to risk in the thrill of the chase. His puffy face, his tubby legs and arms were never without scratches, bruises, welts: marks of the hunt.

Trophies from these expeditions filled his bedroom: obsessively mounted, neatly labelled, under glass, in a dozen drawers and framed boxes. I soon learnt to spell the names and speak the vocabulary, learnt by heart the subtle differences between the Lesser and Greater Fritillary, the Common Yellow and the Lemon Migrant, *Papilio canopus* and *P. fuscus*. Specimens Bennie thought redundant, or flawed in some small way, he would pass on to me. At first I felt an occasional pleasure in capturing—in *owning*—such beauty, but that pleasure soon wore off. And my own efforts at mounting were seldom successful: *my* bedroom soon became littered with dry, brittle butterfly husks and the broken, powdery wings of moths, crunching underfoot.

Much of the time Bennie also had one limb or another— sometimes two—encased in plaster. He had been born to suffer: a favourite victim of school bullies, certainly, but also of all known natural laws and forces. Camped out with him on weekends, I never failed to be amazed as the campfire smoke followed him from compass point to compass point, enveloping him instantly no matter how he tried to elude it.

And slowly I began to find more and more reasons to avoid Bennie, even at weekends.

'You want to sign my plaster?'

'I have to practise.'

'*Please*. No-one wants to sign it.'

'That's not true. Whose signature is that?'

'Mum's.'

'And that?'

'Dad.'

He stood whining in the door of the Music Room, leaning on crutches, his ankle encased in the usual smooth white mass, his glasses so highly polished they seemed—as always—to be empty frames, containing no lenses. I felt an increasing urge to put this to the test, to poke my fingers through . . .

◆

Not till the last drop of rain had been wrung from the last shred of cloud that Wet season was I permitted to play for Keller: the eighth or ninth time I had climbed to his dark room at the *Swan*. The fresher, clearer mornings had softened his heart, perhaps—but only a little.

'Chopin?' I begged.

'We must play Bach before we play Chopin.'

'Which Bach?'

'All of Bach.'

I pulled the Italian Concerto from my shoulder-bag and placed it on the piano, but he laughed. He fossicked among his own music for a few moments, finally emerging with a copy of *The Children's Bach*.

'I played that *years* ago,' I protested.

'You are too proud to play it again?'

'It's easy.'

The moist, red eyes managed to look stern: 'Bach is never easy.'

My father, still attending the occasional lesson, sat scribbling silently in his armchair. *Bach is never easy*. Keller placed the Bach on his piano and began to play. He played the entire book through—a half hour or so—then handed it back.

'No-one can be too proud for this. You will learn each note by next week. Then I will teach you to fit them together. I will teach you the music.'

'Things are happening,' I informed my mother over dinner that night.

'Oh?'

'I've been re-enrolled in kindergarten.'

My father laughed. Nothing seemed able to dent his mood

of late. After tea he unearthed his own copy of *The Children's Bach* and began to play—slowly, taking infinite pains, repeating the simplest of phrases again and again.

'The things he does,' I could hear him saying. 'Listen to this, Nance. And this. The voices. The *nuances*.'

'You don't think they are a bit easy?'

I smiled at his answer: 'Bach is never easy.'

'Of course. But technically . . .'

'He has this ability—finds something new in the most ordinary passage. It's astonishing. You should come to the lessons.'

'I'd melt if I spent another minute in that room.'

'I thought I might perform some of these pieces for the group on Friday night. What do you think?'

'I think they might expect something more difficult.'

'You mean more . . . flashy.'

My parents had eased slowly into the town's social life. With the coming of the Dry—seven months of clear, enamel-blue days—this accelerated. Each weekend brought barbecues, tennis afternoons, gatherings to share drinks, conversation, music . . .

Friday night was 'soirée' night. A circle of amateur musicians, church acquaintances mostly, choir members, began gathering at our house, each taking turns to prepare and perform some piece on piano or flute or vocal chord.

Keller never attended. My father pressed him after each lesson, and at first the maestro made an effort to offer various more or less plausible excuses. Later he merely grunted. Still later, when work commitments prevented my father from attending lessons, I grew weary of inviting him. When asked at home if he would come, I always declined on his behalf.

'He is busy?'

'Feeling unwell,' I would improvise. 'He would love to come, but his ulcer . . .'

'He has an ulcer?'

'I *think* that's what he said. It's hard to tell. The accent . . .'

I performed at those Friday night gatherings myself, once or twice, enjoying the fuss and praise of these teachers and doctors and public servants, basking in an older, more adult acceptance that should have more than compensated for my own age group's rejection.

But didn't.

Discussion on Fridays often turned to the subject of Keller. The First Law of Gossip, my mother liked to call it: always talk about those not present. Various theories, half-truths and slanders were bruited about, often totally contradictory, and always extreme. My own former theory was even aired by others: he was a War Criminal in hiding. More often he was Jewish, an Auschwitz survivor. Or a Russian, a Trotskyite. Sometimes he had a criminal record: postwar black market, forged Deutschmarks. Or he had worked the pearling luggers, made a fortune, filtered it through his kidneys . . .

'How long has he been here?' My father was always curious.

'Ten years, at least.'

'Nearer fifteen. Why, I remember . . .'

Such approximations added little to the informal dossier my parents had managed to compile. His prewar European fame—an article of faith now with my father—surprised everyone: certainly none of the natives had heard him play in public.

My father defended him. 'He was a pupil of Leschetizky,' he declared, with reverence.

When this rang no bells, he felt compelled to expand: 'Who of course was a pupil of Liszt.'

But even this provided no immunity.

'There are pupils and there are pupils,' my mother murmured.

All their conversation ceased. I always marvelled at this power of hers: how she could always gain attention by lowering her voice.

'Remember the story of Mascagni,' she reminded my father, then turned to the rest of the gathering. 'The Italian composer?'

'You mean Mas*canyi*?' The church organist, a relentless know-all, corrected her pronunciation. 'Composer of *Cavalleria Rusticana*?'

'Probably,' my mother smiled, unruffled. 'Whoever. The composer passed some organ-grinder in the street, grinding out a tune from his new opera. He stopped briefly to explain to the grinder that it should be played more rapidly.'

She paused to offer the cheese dip around, maintaining the suspense.

'Next time he passed that way a sign was hung on the barrel of the organ: Pupil of Mascagni.'

Even my father laughed, before insisting:

'Keller is no organ-grinder.'

The church organist—I remember she always pronounced it *organiste*—admitted taking lessons, briefly, from the maestro some years before; but only lasting four weeks:

'He didn't teach me a thing.'

Listening to her play in church each Sunday, I suspected that Keller would have echoed those words, if with a slightly different emphasis.

———— ◆ ————

The Dry season ran its seemingly endless course: a perma-spring of perfect weather, each day a high, blue transparency; each night cloudless and cool, and between the two the narrowest littoral of twilight—the sun high in the sky one minute, the next gone, sucked suddenly, silently below the horizon.

Our evening meals had moved outside onto the balcony: a nightly cooling ritual before re-entering the warmer house for music and homework.

Keller also had moved outside. Each Tuesday I would find him sitting in the beer garden, downstairs, as if the Dry had somehow made him more sociable, more democratic. His white suit and Panama could not be missed among the blue singlets and short-sleeved shirts; the clear, heavy fluid of his schnapps bottle likewise, standing high and separate among the amber, lathered beers.

As I entered he would rise and follow me up the stairs,

already talking music. His recall of where we had left off the week before was always total.

'Have you finished the Rondo?'

'Half-finished.'

'That is not possible.'

'I'm sorry?'

'Is water at fifty degrees half-boiling?'

He was full of such advice, fragments of folk wisdom that had a vaguely oriental flavour to them.

'What is the difference between good and great pianists?' he often asked, as I came close to whatever musical essence he was seeking—close, but always achingly just out of reach.

I would shrug.

'Not much,' he would murmur, and a small smile might be permitted to play momentarily around his dry lips. 'Just a little.'

That last 'littleness' was impossible to bridge: a tiny gulf that was the sum of a thousand infinitesimal differences.

'Always the most difficult part of a race,' he paraphrased himself, 'is the last step.'

I would play a page, a phrase, a single bar again and again—following where he led, on his own keyboard, until he finally shrugged:

'Perhaps there can be no perfection. Only levels of imperfection. Only . . . differences. Each time we move closer and closer—but can never be satisfied. A piece is never complete, only at some stage abandoned.'

I would return again the next week, ignoring his advice, determinedly seeking something final, inviolate, satisfying. I would play till my hands ached and he lifted them from the keyboard and chided me gently:

'We must know when to move on. To search too long for perfection can also paralyse.'

I wondered then if he was telling me not to bother—not to try too hard. I wondered if he had set some lower level for me, without telling me: some lower step on the dais that would be . . . sufficient.

The idea infuriated me. At home, and at school during

lunchhours, I redoubled my efforts to defy the theory of limits and approach ever more closely—and finally grasp—the ideal I was sure he felt me incapable of reaching.

———— ♦ ————

*A*t school I was falling in love.

Megan's desk stood in front of mine, and perhaps it was her back that I first loved: the furred nape of her neck, her smooth bare shoulders, the thick cumulus of pale hair. The late afternoon light streamed through the western windows, diffracting softly through the edges of that hair and around the downy edges of her skin. By Home Time each day she became a haloed vision.

That vision lodged deeply inside me, especially the glowing hair. It was the feel of her soft, thick hair that woke me one late May morning, hard and pulsing below the waist, the bedsheets sticky with a strange pale honey, the first I'd seen.

The glow of that first coming stayed with me all morning, carrying me through long hours of Maths and Physics and Modern History. I was lost to the world of ideas—lifted to some high hormonal plateau, feeling manly, invulnerable, immensely content.

At lunch, filled with love, or lust, remembering the feel of that dream hair, I abandoned the Music Room to seek out Megan in a corner of the covered area, interrupting her lunch with a rambling, foot-shuffling monologue that wound in ever-narrowing circles to one final, awkward sentence: Will You Come To The Pictures With Me On Saturday Night?

She smiled. She might have been opening a piano: a wide keyboard of white, perfect teeth.

'I'm already going, Paul.'

'Next week, then?'

She shook her head, still smiling. 'It was sweet of you to ask.'

The Sweet of the world, I knew instinctively, did not make lovers. The Sweet could aim no higher than a kind of honorary girlishness that carried the label just Good Friends.

'I dreamt about you last night,' I blurted out, unable to look her in the eyes, but wanting to shock, wanting to be anything but sweet.

She laughed: 'How was I?'

'What?'

'Was I good?'

'I didn't mean . . .'

She slipped her arm behind my neck, stood tiptoe and kissed me briefly on the lips.

'You can have me in dreams anytime,' she murmured. 'But that's the only place.'

This blunt talk so thrilled me that I failed for some minutes to hear the message. Those various demure girlfriends whose sweaty palms I'd clutched in the South, or Queen's Waltzed cheek-to-cheek at School Socials, could never have spoken like this.

'I already have a man,' she said. The sophisticated sound of the word—completely foreign to the schoolyard lexicon of Boyfriends and Steadies—excited me further.

'Who is it?' I called; but she was already walking away.

Jimmy Papas, a school tough in the class ahead of me, was waiting in the bike shed after school that night. Short, thickset, wire-haired, he did not look happy. He had been waiting a long time: in a fury of rejection I had hammered away at Czerny in the Music Room for an hour, punishing myself for being myself.

'You been bothering Megan Murray?'

'Who told you that? Megan?'

His face was set in a sneer that I always thought reserved for me. Later I realised it was a fixture. His best friends received that same look. His dog received it. His *breakfast* received it.

'Scotty told me. And Megan belongs to Scotty. You keep away.'

He grabbed me by the shirt-front. Buttons popped.

'Hope you've got a needle and thread,' I tried recklessly

to joke. Or perhaps I felt I needed further punishment.

'Fucking poofter,' he shoved me backwards into an empty bike rack. 'Not worth a punch. You want to play with yourself do it in private. Just keep away from Megan.'

He began to walk away; but once again my mouth, always a dangerous weapon, autonomous to some extent, got the better of me:

'I thought I was doing you a favour.'

He turned, puzzled: 'What do you mean?'

'With Megan out of the way you'd have Scotty all to yourself.'

'You don't learn, do you?' he shouted, enraged.

The ride home that afternoon was the longest I ever made. My torn shirt flapped in the slipstream, my nose bled, I ached, nauseous with pain. The dreamy high of the morning had gone.

'What happened?' my mother demanded.

If Darwin High School was a prison, quarantined on its headland, then the Law of the prison yard applied. This I knew by some ancient instinct.

'Fell off,' I lied.

'I want the truth, Paul. If you are being victimised . . .'

'That *is* the truth.'

My father was not so concerned.

'A few fights won't do him any harm,' he laughed. 'I was always fighting at school. Boys like to fight.'

'But what about his *hands*?' my mother persisted.

'Mine survived,' he said, seating himself at the piano.

'But *look* at him. He's covered in bruises. His nose might be broken.'

My father turned to me, smiling. 'What does the other bloke look like?'

'Worse,' I lied again, surprised to find that the idea of me fighting impressed him, and deciding to take this easy way out. Perhaps he was merely being his usual contrary self—putting the other side of the argument.

'Good,' he said. 'You stand up for your rights.'

I woke the next morning sticky again, and warm and wetly

contented in the groin, and Megan—at least—forgiven. I was sure she had not meant me to be beaten. And even if she *had* I could have forgiven her: the glow of those moist, throbbing dreams surrounded and protected her—a glow as real and warm as the nimbus of golden sunlight that enveloped her each afternoon as she stood between me and the window to pack her bag . . .

'Sweet dreams,' she often teased as she left, tossing her bag across one shoulder and walking out, skirt twitching.

I liked to think that it excited her, just a little, the knowledge that someone was dreaming of her, sexually. I liked to imagine that home in her bed she could sense in *her* dreams what was happening in mine.

Which was plenty: at the end of the week my bedsheets were stiff enough to stand against the wall. And my mother, who changed those sheets, looked at me differently: with a kind of worried amusement, or concerned pride, although nothing was ever said.

——— ◆ ———

'*I*sn't He Talented,' my parents never tired of hearing their friends remark.

I played a small piece or two most Friday nights, basking afterwards in the murmurs of appreciation.

'Isn't He Coming On Nicely.'

'You Must Be So Proud.'

One voice was always missing from this chorus of praise: my teacher's. For this I blamed the instrument he allowed me to play: the *Wertheim* upright, its ivory keys chipped and yellowed and peeling, its action stiff and unpredictable, corroded by the humidity. *His* piano—the *Bösendorfer* 'supine'—contained some sort of heat lamp suspended among the strings to dispel moisture, lending an eerie violet glow to the instrument, and at times also to his face as he sat above it. Apparently he felt the upright to be beyond such tendernesses.

'Make music on that,' he told me. 'And you can make music on anything.'

'It gets worse every week.'

'Far worse to learn on a perfect instrument,' he answered. 'And then adjust to this.'

'But I played this piece much better at home,' I tried to persuade him. 'Yesterday.'

The keyboard was uneven, and the mechanisms had a life of their own—but at least the upright was always in tune. He possessed his own set of tools—a small black doctor's bag of oddly shaped spanners and tuning forks, and he kept both instruments harmonised. Even the slightest discordance would have been unthinkable: every phrase I played on my piano was echoed on his.

His echoes were always an immense improvement, and this also—in my youthful arrogance—I decided was mechanical. Of *course* he sounded better: he had the better piano.

The chance to prove my theory, if only to myself, came one June afternoon. I arrived at the *Swan* to find no sign of Keller, either in his room or in the bar below. His door had been left ajar, presumably for me. Entering, I sat myself for the first time at the grand, breaking his strict rule. Keeping a sharp ear cocked for the approach of footsteps, I played for some time, enjoying the freedom of a keyboard that not so much resisted the hands as allowed the music to shine through, a keyboard that might have been made of clear water or transparent glass.

As I played, the hinged frame of photographs—an ornamental silver clamshell—that Keller kept propped on his piano caught my eye. Often I had seen his gaze stray there during lessons, but never had I been close enough to follow the direction of that gaze.

One wing of the clam held a faded, grainy family portrait: a young plumpish woman, seated, a child standing next to her, and behind both what could only be a much younger version of Keller, his firm, proprietorial arm resting on the shoulder of the woman.

All three subjects stared into the camera with an awed, awkward seriousness—photography always seemed a Serious Business in those early days.

Which made me curious: how early was it? I'd seen such serious group photographs before in the albums of my grandparents—photographs from the first couple of decades of the century. The clothing here seemed to come from an even earlier age, however. Sunday Best, perhaps—Sunday Best always harks nostalgically to earlier, more formal times—but there was something even older, something almost historical in the woman's white blouse, throat-brooch, full-length dark skirt. The child—gender uncertain, probably a girlish boy—was dressed in a stylised sailor costume. And Keller? Dark suit, wing collar, his serious eyes staring over the pince-nez sitting affectedly on his nose.

The other wing of the frame contained a different photograph: an even younger Keller, in a lighter suit and less formal collar, seated at a piano; the same woman—plump, full-bosomed—this time standing behind him, her arms resting on his shoulders, her face half-turned to the camera, her mouth a perfect O of song.

The music spread on the piano stand in that grainy photograph was of course impossible to decipher. I slipped the photograph from the frame and found a handful of faded words scribbled on the back: *Habe Dank*, and a placename and date, later than I expected: *Salzburg, Oktober, '27.*

And then I jumped, startled, as the door opened behind me. The hinged frame of the photographs almost slipped from my hand. Why is it always at the exact moment of slaking curiosity that we are caught, stickybeaked?

'Good afternoon,' the familiar voice came from the open door.

'Good afternoon, maestro.'

I had never called him Adolf to his face. Now, even behind his back, the title 'maestro' seemed somehow natural.

'You have been playing without permission?' he asked.

'Just looking. I didn't know what to do.'

I carefully placed the photographs back on the piano and

returned to my rightful place at the upright.

'Your family?' I ventured.

'*Those* are my family,' he murmured, gesturing at the shelves of sheet music.

And that was that: after a brief apology for his lateness—a doctor's appointment—the lesson proceeded as normally as any lesson was capable of proceeding.

As I left, however, he turned and called after me:

'My son's name was Eric. My wife, Mathilde.'

I slunk down the stairs, half-shamed but half-excited by my discoveries. He had never before talked of himself during lessons. Nor, it seemed, did he talk of himself *out* of lessons: my parents had learnt nothing from their multiple enquiries. Even the letters my father had written to various acquaintances in the South—musicians, librarians—had drawn minimal returns.

'Perhaps his wife and child died in the War,' my mother suggested when I told her about the photographs.

My own theory appealed more:

'Perhaps they left him. After a piano lesson.'

She laughed: 'Let's be serious.'

My father now took no part in our speculations. He pretended to be no longer interested in solving the great mystery of Eduard Keller. From time to time he would suggest that the man had a right to privacy, to freedom from gossip. But he too wished to know more: that single listing of the name Keller in the Music Dictionary under Leschetizky still teased at him, excited him. When the subject arose on Tuesday nights, after lessons, the paper he was ostensibly reading would dip slightly, or else his book would remain at the same page, unturned for minutes, as he listened to us talk.

'His wife was a singer,' I told my mother. 'Mathilde.'

'Famous?'

'I don't know. Chances are. Shall we look her up?'

'Probably useless. She would have kept her maiden name as a professional singer. But let's try.'

'They were in a place called Salzburg in 1927,' I remembered.

My father laughed from behind the shelter of his headlines: 'So no doubt was every other musician in Europe at some time during the year 1927. You'll have to do better than that.'

Nevertheless, I saw another envelope lying on the table among the mail to be posted the following morning, marked: AIRMAIL. It was addressed to one of his musical contacts in the South.

He, too, still burned with curiosity.

———— ◆ ————

*T*hat June an extra evening was added to my parents' weekly musical calendar: Gilbert and Sullivan night. More musical gipsies than Doctor and Doctor's Wife, they had left a trail of Gilbert and Sullivan performances across the South— a different operetta in every town in which we lived. From an early age I also was involved, if only in lesser, supporting roles. By early teens I had played a pirate in *Penzance*, a courtier in *The Mikado*, a juror in *Trial By* . . .

That simple, stylised music saturates my earliest memories: music first heard from a bassinet beneath my mother's piano in various small-town Institutes or Church Halls as she rehearsed the chorus, the squeak of her foot on a pedal close to my ear.

From this my infallible rhythmic sense?

My first memories of my father are of rhythm too: his figure, nearby, arms raised, slicing the air into bars of music as she played. Medicine was his job, music his life. Or—as he often paraphrased his favourite writer, the Russian Chekhov— medicine was his wife, music his mistress.

Which was wonderful, and terrible. I still remember Christmas mornings as a child, rising in the half-dark before dawn, my hands fumbling in a stuffed pillowslip, trying to comprehend with excited fingers the rough braille of those wrapped, mysterious gifts.

A football? An . . . electric train?

As I grew older, guesswork became unnecessary: the bundles

were always instantly recognisable by touch. My father's father had died when he was young. He had no role model. I think he innocently believed that every father gave his ten-year-old son a bound Busoni edition of *The Well Tempered Clavier* in his Christmas stocking. And, the following Christmas, Schnabel's eccentric readings of the Beethoven *Sonatas*.

But Gilbert and Sullivan came first. Music was only part of it. As Opening Night approached, costumes were endlessly sewn or sequined by my mother after meals at night. Stage sets were assembled in backyards by teams of art teachers and amateur watercolourists every weekend; facsimile Venetian canals or Japanese gardens glued and nailed together out of plywood and cardboard and masonite.

Certain pungent glue smells still transport me back to the kitchen where I watched, aged four, as various hand-painted half-moons of rice paper were painstakingly stuck by my mother to tiny bird-boned wooden skeletons: folding fans for *The Mikado*. Her exquisite stage props were often fashioned even more carefully than the objects they represented: Art not so much imitating as improving upon Life.

That first year in Darwin the choice was *HMS Pinafore*. Auditions were held, mostly in our lounge around the piano, and roles parcelled out among the members of the Musical Society. My father, after a week of hard lobbying, found himself in the role of Major General; my mother as always was on piano, the engine-room of the production.

And suddenly it was hard to find practice time at home as she hogged the instrument, endlessly rehearsing her Overture and accompaniment. She was the finest sight-reader I have known—but like many sight-readers her memory was faulty, unpractised. She needed the piano more than me. And there were rehearsals to attend, and costume measurements, and I seemed to arrive at the *Swan* each Tuesday unprepared, further and further behind . . .

'You have done nothing this week.'

'I have no time.'

'There is no point in repeating our last consultation.'

'You expect too much.'

'I expect very little. You are free not to practise. Of course. And free also not to attend.'

'I never hear _you_ practise.'

He smiled: 'Only those who are dirty need to wash.'

Suffering such humiliations might have been worthwhile if my part in the opera that year was larger. But once again I found myself lost in the chorus: a Marine hidden deep inside a platoon of older, larger Marines.

'Your voice hasn't broken properly,' my father claimed.

'Has so!' I growled, deeply.

'You don't even shave every day.'

'I _do_ so!'

But here my anger betrayed me, control lapsed, my voice reverting to a high furious mouse-squeak.

I juggled my commitments over the next two months, cutting corners, cycling desperately back and forth across town after school, frequently managing to be in two places at once. Or so it seems now: the weeks telescoped into one long frantic blur of days and events that ended suddenly, abruptly, on the morning of Opening Night when I awoke into a Saturday of immense, anxious emptiness.

'Never practise on the day of a performance,' my father was already telling my mother over breakfast, his chair placed physically between her and the piano, blocking access, the lid of the instrument locked, the key hidden away.

'But the Overture . . . the left hand needs work.'

'The left hand will be fine.'

'Please, John. Just a few mintues.'

They played this familiar game all day; a game of ritual fun at first, but as the hours passed becoming more serious, more tense. We left home absurdly early that evening: my mother fidgeting, agitated, already wiping her sweating palms on a piece of towelling, wanting at least to _be_ at the hall, doing something, even if only selling tickets.

'Sitting in the anxious seat,' my father teased, using a phrase he had brought home from Keller which had amused them both and entered our family dialect.

'I'm not at all anxious.'

'You're shaking all over.'

'I must be cold.'

'In *this* climate?'

'Maybe I am a *little* bit worried.'

'Relax.'

'What if I lose my place. What if . . .'

'You won't. You never do.'

'Look: I'm trembling like a leaf.'

'The adrenalin. It's good for you. You don't look at all nervous.'

Only after the performance did she relax: entering a serene, untouchable trance, a deep satisfaction that lasted till the morning before the next performance.

My father was more in his element: strutting the stage in a parody uniform and a kilogram of jingling medals, singing absurd songs at breakneck speed, bathing himself in the laughter and applause. At these times—and afterwards, kite-high on excitement—he bore no resemblance remotely to anyone I knew. I suspected I was glimpsing some part of him that had long been repressed: some frivolous, joyous core that hardship, childhood tragedy and the War had buried inside him too long.

Half-filled with love, half with envy, I knew that I, too, wanted the spotlight. Centre-stage. Up front.

With the opera over I redoubled my efforts at the keyboard. If Keller asked for two Bach fugues each week, I prepared three. If he required three hours' practice, I played for four . . .

'Work makes free,' he would often tell me, smiling grimly as if at some private joke.

——— ◆ ———

The champagne cork popped upwards, passed neatly through the blades of the revolving fan, rebounded from the ceiling and passed down through the blades again, unscathed, as if synchronised.

My parents laughed at this minor miracle. Even Keller managed a small, tight smile.

'Here's to a wonderful talent,' my father proposed, pouring out the creamy, foaming liquid.

'Here's to talent . . . properly harnessed,' my mother added as she tilted her glass in the direction of Keller.

'Here's to a technical hurdle safely negotiated.' As he limited his toast he sipped primly, his mouth tight and wrinkled, a dried fruit.

Late August, for my sixteenth birthday, he had finally accepted a dinner invitation. And it was clear he was not going out of his way to secure another.

The dinner was a double celebration: my Associate results from the Music Board had arrived from the South: A+, a rare and amazing result. Both parents were thrilled—agreed for once in this—but Keller remained unmoved, outwardly at least. His presence that night was the sole evidence of any pride he might share in my—our?—achievement.

Or had he come for the opposite reason? To douse the festivities with cold water lest they get out of hand?

'Such an exam means nothing,' he shrugged. 'Who was the examiner?'

'But an A *plus*?'

'The boy is too given to self-satisfaction. The self-satisfied go no further.'

My mother tried to tease him. 'But surely you must be just a *little* bit pleased?'

'Am I pleased,' Keller asked, 'because it is Friday? Because it is eight o'clock? Exams are a technical hurdle only. A chronological hurdle: a ticking of the clock. A sign that time is passing.'

My parents exchanged the first of many winks I was to witness behind his back that night—winks augmented by a sign language of ever-increasing sophistication: raised eyebrows, discreetly rolled eyes, fingers pressed to hushing lips.

'Well *we're* in the mood for celebrating,' my father pronounced. 'And I propose a toast to you maestro, for all the hard work you have put in.'

After the second bottle Keller began—just a little—to loosen up.

'Fine wine,' he murmured. 'Imported?'

'Barossa Valley,' my father told him, grateful for the cue, able to launch into his usual wine monologue: part South Australian pride, part Trivial Pursuit, part travelogue.

'You should visit,' he recommended as he finished his winding, verbal tour of the Barossa vineyards. 'Many of the older folk still speak German. The culture is very strong.'

'I am Austrian,' Keller said.

More eye and sign language passed between my parents—pitched at some frequency they seemed to believe beyond his range of hearing.

'Of course,' my mother said. 'But you *speak* German. It's part of the same culture.'

'Someone else thought that,' Keller murmured. 'Thirty years ago.'

Silence followed. Small talk was impossible with this man. We watched him watching his wine: his weather-beaten face had taken on a regular, corrugated appearance, as if concentrating, deep in thought.

'Terrible things happened here during the War too,' my mother eventually resumed, trying to correct her mistake but only adding to it. 'German placenames were changed. Composers were banned: even Beethoven. German speakers were interned . . .'

'One presumes they were not gassed,' Keller murmured. 'And then burnt, after the removal of gold amalgam.'

He spoke so mildly, so matter-of-factly, that it was impossible to tell if he were rebuking her or making some sort of horrific joke.

'You don't play in public,' she said, changing the subject after another short, deep silence. 'Anymore.'

'I am too lazy, dear lady.'

'But such a talent.'

He laughed, mockingly: 'You have perhaps heard me?'

'You learnt from Theodore Leschetizky,' my father prompted.

Keller glanced at him curiously, then shrugged.

'Very briefly,' he said. 'I was not a good student.'

The wall was up again.

'Is it your finger?' I put in, trying to crudely lever the bricks from that wall—and able, I knew, to hide my brashness behind the excuse of youth and innocence.

He waggled the stump of his finger in front of me.

'There are concert pianists with one whole hand missing,' he smiled. 'What is one little finger?'

'I just thought . . .'

'The ear-finger, we call it at home.'

He jammed the stump into the socket of his ear and agitated furiously.

'*This* is my problem: I can no longer clean my ear.'

And he laughed for the first time that night—uproariously, harshly.

'Shall we eat?' my mother rose from the couch. 'We're having Wiener Schnitzel tonight, Herr Keller. In your honour. And sauerkraut—I had awful trouble finding a recipe. I hope it doesn't make you homesick . . .'

'Nothing, dear lady, could make me homesick.'

'You must miss the musical life. The orchestras.'

He snorted: 'So many ponderous orchestras and so much ponderous music. I miss nothing.'

'Vienna,' she continued, determined, 'is my favourite foreign city. I only know it from photographs, of course. The Spanish Riding School. The Ringstrasse . . .'

'The Ringstrasse,' he snorted again. 'Of course. An excellent city for military pomp and processions.'

'But such beautiful architecture.'

'Movie-set architecture,' he murmured. 'Ornamental facades. Hiding the hypocrisy within . . .'

He seemed more talkative after his ear-finger joke, but there were no further self-revelations. The conversation stumbled fitfully, awkwardly from Vienna to wine to music, to music written about wine, to the climate, to the food, and lastly to me.

'Perhaps you could play one of the exam pieces, Paul,' my

father suggested. 'A private concert for the three of us.'

'The Brahms?'

'The Beethoven,' Keller interjected, 'might be preferable.'

I played Beethoven that night as well as I had ever played, and turned afterwards, smiling, ready for praise.

'Beautiful,' my mother breathed. 'Don't you agree, Herr Keller?'

'An excellent forgery,' he said.

'I'm sorry?'

'Technically perfect,' he said.

He drained his wineglass before continuing. It was to be his longest monologue of the evening:

'At such moments I always remember a forged painting I once saw. In a museum in Amsterdam: Van Gogh. A fascinating art work. Each violent brushstroke was reproduced with painstaking, non-violent care. The forgery must have taken many *many* times longer than the original to complete. It was technically *better* than the original.'

He rose from his chair and walked a little unsteadily towards the door: 'And yet something was missing. Not much—but *something*.'

At the door he paused, and turned: 'And that small something may as well have been everything.'

He bowed slightly: 'Thankyou, dear lady, for your hospitality.'

His mouth uttered the conventional words, but his face remained dead, unsmiling. *That* was the forgery, I decided, not my Beethoven: a forgery of good manners.

Or perhaps all manners were a kind of forgery.

'Please,' he continued. 'Do not rise from your stools. I can walk. The boy may consult me again on Tuesday.'

——— ◆ ———

Throughout October the sky slowly thickened and bloated, the atmosphere grew weighty, super-saturated with moisture and trapped heat. The transparent air of the Dry—

46

a cool absence—became a presence: something that resisted movement and breath, that rubbed against the skin like hot liniment, that could be touched and felt and always, endlessly, discussed.

The town beneath remained dry and dusty, its earth somehow growing even drier as its inhabitants grew damp: thin, wet claddings of dust sticking to each sweating patch of skin.

'The season of raised voices and heat rashes,' my father pronounced. 'The season of tropical sores and family disputes.'

Once again he began bringing home horror stories every night from work: anecdotes from the life of a busy doctor in Darwin, forced to work harder than he wished. I was never quite sure if this was due to the effect of the Wet on his patients, or on him. Always a connoisseur of the human comedy, those humid months deepened his amusement into morbid obsession.

Mostly the stories were classified Adults Only, for Restricted Listening: but as my parents lay in bed, talking behind a shut door, their voices often carried out through the open louvres and through the humid stillness outside the house, re-entering again through my windows.

'He'd tied some sort of rubber band around the base, then couldn't get it off. Wanted a permanent erection. The tip was already gangrenous.'

'How terrible.'

'We managed to save two-thirds.'

'Well, you know what I always say,' my mother murmured. 'It isn't how much you've got . . .'

They laughed softly together, perhaps the best defence they had been able to develop over the years, but I was not yet so immune to human stupidity. Squirming in bed, trying not to listen but unable not to hear, I found it hard to place these squalid stories in the same world as the Mozart K. 576 or 332 my father might have played only minutes before, or the limpid, watery Debussy that my mother liked to splash into the air as if to cool us in the heat of the evening.

'Her lover died on top of her. Heart attack. She came in the ambulance with the body.'

'She must have been very upset.'

He snorted: 'More angry than upset.'

'With him?'

'All she could talk about was his car keys. Where the hell were they? His car was still parked in her drive—and she wanted it moved before her husband got home.'

'Pretty cool customer.'

'Said she didn't realise he was having a heart attack. He always made a lot of noise coming.'

'And going.'

The town waited, knife edged, for the abscess of the heavens to burst and bring at least partial relief, but the stories continued even more thickly into November: a month the locals like to speak of—with a kind of odd, perverse pride—as the Suicide Month.

'Saw a strange one today. Shut himself in his garage with two cars, with both motors running.'

'*Both*? Why both?'

'I don't know. Perhaps one car could be an accident. Two is a statement. A kind of suicide note.'

'He had two cars?'

'Borrowed his girlfriend's.'

As the world grew hotter, and the louvred walls of the houses were cranked open to maximum aperture, all privacy vanished. To walk the streets at night was to walk among rows of lined, illuminated screens, as if at some vast drive-in—a supermarket of drive-ins. A constant soundtrack of country and western music filled the air: plangent ballads of love, jealousy, murder and jail spilling out of the high, opened houses and pubs. Across each screen—raised on stilts above the shrubbery, louvres wide open—even the most fantastic stories my father related suddenly seemed possible, and visible.

In the entire town perhaps only the wooden slats of Eduard Keller's bedroom remained closed. Climbing the stairs to his shuttered room each Tuesday, I was able to tell myself I was finally beginning to gain some sort of understanding of the man. The *Swan* was a monastery, of a kind: a place of retreat, of renunciation of the world. A place for atonement—against all the evidence, I still thought him guilty of war crimes— a place for examination of the heart.

And examination of the liver, also, certainly. A place of *partial* renunciation. His bottle of schnapps was never more than arm's length distance.

The November humidity seemed to draw out his worst, exaggerate his faults, and render him a caricature of himself. His face reddened further, his moist lids drooped—there was even the occasional crease in his starched white suit. I would find him each steamy Tuesday hunched in his dark room, brooding, the schnapps bottle always at his elbow, his fat scrapbook of newspaper clippings once again before him . . .

In this, he resembled my father: the Wet brought out a morbid, brooding curiosity in the doings of his fellow humans. Those scrapbooks would be in his hands as I arrived, and he would be reaching for them again as I left. I could only presume he spent the entire time between lessons gazing at clippings. I remembered those movies I often saw as a child in the South, on holidays in the city: movies which screened continuously, beginning again as soon as they ended . . .

So Keller in his humid room stared endlessly at his clippings, turning back to the first page as he reached the last, as if trying to fit them together into some new version of events, perhaps even hoping for some variation, some change, some different ending. I began to plan how I could get my hands on them, discover exactly *what* was so fascinating.

His teaching methods also changed with the coming of the Wet: suddenly he seemed to find the music of certain composers unbearable, no matter how well I played.

'Leave it for now.'

'But I practised especially . . .'

'It is insincere. So much . . . showing off.'

'My playing?'

'The music.'

As the humidity climbed, his musical taste narrowed sharply, his choice of pieces retreated further into the past—to Beethoven first, then back to Mozart and deeper still to Bach,

Scarlatti, and finally just scales and more scales, as if seeking some kind of ultimate discipline, some perfect control to set against the treacheries of emotion.

'But the Rachmaninoff is so beautiful.'

His hackles rose: 'We must be on our guard against beauty always. Never trust the beautiful.'

'But beauty is what music is *for.*'

I could never follow this strange line of argument. I sat, twitching restlessly on my stool, hands fidgeting, longing to play as he tried, stumbling, to explain.

'Beauty simplifies,' he said. 'The best music is neither beautiful nor ugly. Like the world, it is infinitely complex. Full of nuance. Rich beyond any reduction. We must not make the mistake of confusing music with emotion.'

Throughout the hot, wet month of November any kind of emotional expression was forbidden, *verboten*: Mozart was played in the manner of Bach, and Bach in the manner of scales, according to strict metronomic markings.

'Music is a kind of arithmetic,' he told me.

And again, as I pressed him to allow me to return to my then favourites—to Liszt and Rachmaninoff, to noise and speed and blurred hands and lyric flashiness.

'If you want people to believe your lies,' he grunted, 'set them to music.'

Intermezzo

We fled south for several weeks that Christmas, arriving in Adelaide at the home of my grandparents, my mother's parents, after a five-day drive.

Of that interminable trip only odd dream images remain: a water sprinkler twinkling on a postage stamp of lawn somewhere in the desert; the sky for miles black with clouds of thirsty budgerigars; a taxi heading south into that same desert, pulling over at some arranged spot and disgorging its passenger—a bearded black tribesman who paid his fare and strode off into the hot dunes, barefoot, carrying nothing but spears.

And then we were through the desert and into the temperate wheat country, passing through the mid-north towns in which I had once lived—centuries ago, in an earlier life, it now seemed. The closer we approached to Adelaide, the slower our journey became, stopping more and more frequently in those small wheat-belt towns, visiting old friends, reliving past Gilbert and Sullivan triumphs . . .

Until finally, somehow, we reached the City itself.

As a child, growing up in the bush, I was always aware of that distant presence. There was only one City, it seemed then: a far-off magical place always spoken of in hushed tones, and always spelled with a capital. School holidays, then as now, above all else meant a trip to the City, and an extended stay with grandparents of limitless generosity and tolerance and time up their sleeves. The City meant Television, of course—but there were other joys that still remain in my mind in a sort of mental upper-case, and usually preceded by the definite article, as befits magical things. The Zoo, and the Beach. The Glenelg Tram. The Show, and its attendant subdivisions of joy: Show Bags, Ghost Trains, Ferris Wheels. The Museum—especially its crypt-like Egyptian Room, full of mummies, sarcophagi, mysterious inscriptions and other graveyard loot.

Holidays also meant the Pictures—not yet become the Movies—and long afternoons of Batman, Tarzan, Fantales and Jaffas . . .

Those childhood pleasures had lost some of their joy for me by the age of sixteen, but this took time to discover.

I posted a Christmas card to the *Swan* between trips to the Beach: a European scene of falling snow and bare birches and candle-lit windows, something I hoped might bring a little coolness into Keller's steamy room. I was a little surprised to receive a card, and a crude bachelor-wrapped parcel, in return.

Kind Regards to Your Family. Do no Neglect the Czerny: three studies a day.

My mother was highly amused:

'Feel flattered, Paul. Those words are the nearest he can get to saying he misses you.'

We unwrapped the gift: a battered, yellowing edition of Czerny, the Opus 599 studies.

'I've already got this,' I said, disappointed.

My father was carefully examining the flyleaf:

'Not *this* edition.'

He beckoned my mother:

'Look at the date. Might even be a first edition.'

They scrutinised the markings, and turned a page:

'A *signed* first edition,' they discovered, together.

'Must be worth a fortune,' my father murmured. 'And he sends it two thousand miles wrapped in a scrap of grocer's paper.'

'Perhaps that was the only way he could give it,' she suggested. 'At a distance. Carelessly. As if it meant nothing.'

That signed first edition, 150–odd years old, whetted my curiosity. I had been ordered out of the sun for several days, my face and shoulders blistered. Bored—finally—with daytime Television, and my pocket money reserves running too low for further trips to The Pictures, I began visiting libraries, searching for evidence of Keller's earlier life. My father was always busy—unable to holiday, he spent those weeks at his parents' piano, or at hospital refresher courses, lectures, and ward rounds—but my mother, a former librarian, often accompanied me, guiding me through arcane numbering systems, catalogues, indexes. Finding nothing in any of the nearby suburban libraries, she let me loose into the book-lined labyrinths of the Barr-Smith Library at Adelaide University. I spent much of my remaining school holiday there, the Beach and Television forgotten as I pored through biographies, textbooks, histories of pianism, following a faint, erratic trail of Dewey breadcrumbs through the maze from shelves 786.00—*Pianism*—to 943.6—*History of the Austro-Hungarian Empire*—and back again.

We had the library to ourselves; no-one seemed to visit those dark, dusty corners. And perhaps no-one ever had: certain back stacks of the library seemed unvisited, left off the maps, accidentally omitted, perhaps, from updated catalogues. Whole shelves of books could be found which had not been borrowed for twenty years. Whole days could pass without sighting another living being between shelves 943.6 and 944.

For a few brief weeks that summer the two of us must have known more about the history of music in Vienna than anyone else on the face of the planet. It formed the raw material for an informal quiz game we played endlessly in the tram home, or en route to the concerts that my parents were determined to cram into their holiday every night.

'How many of his pupils did Theodore Leschetizky marry?'
'Four?'
'Incorrect. He was married four times, yes—but only three times to pupils. My turn to ask again. In what month of what year was Stefan Askenaze's debut in Vienna?'

We did not learn a great deal about the history of Eduard Keller. Small gleanings came to light occasionally, transcribed instantly into a notebook to share with my father that night—but we discovered little more than we already knew. Three books gave his birthdate: a year we had not known, but guessed at, 1887. One book also gave the date of his death: 1944. A strange chill passed through me on reading this.

My mother gave it no significance, a simple error.

'I think we may safely assume that Herr Keller is still alive.'

On the possibility that his wife had been a well-known singer, this lead we also followed—but no Mathilde Keller could be found. I assumed my mother's guess to be correct—Mathilde had used her maiden name professionally.

The breakthrough came one late summer afternoon: a footnote buried in a biography of Richard Strauss, the great Bavarian composer. I was alone: towards the end of the holidays my mother had grown increasingly tired of the search and found better things to do. My own interest had only grown, my scope of inquiry slowly widening, a ripple of curiosity spreading from Vienna to engulf Salzburg, and then finally crossing the border into Germany itself. Knowledge was a kind of drug, I had discovered: it could as easily be pursued for its own sake as for tracking down the elusive Keller. One bibliography led to another, and another . . .

Strauss's Jewish daughter-in-law, I idly read, was able to remain in his household, in Germany, ungassed and uncremated, throughout the War. But it was the small footnote to this passage which electrified me, lifted me straight out of a lazy summer afternoon torpor and carried me to the nearest public phone and my mother's ear:

Strauss's daughter-in-law was more fortunate than some. Marriage to the Austrian pianist Eduard Keller could not save the celebrated Jewish contralto and Wagner specialist, Mathilde Rosenthal, who died in Auschwitz, probably in 1942.

There was no mention of the child—Eric—in that tiny, enormously charged footnote. And no mention of Keller himself.

We discussed this find endlessly that night, and I tossed restlessly in bed for much of the night thinking it through.

In the morning, however, at the library, I was to learn things far more urgent and exciting . . . and all thought of Keller vanished from my head.

Engrossed in tracking further footnotes I failed to hear the footsteps tiptoeing in the next aisle: the two pairs of footsteps.

Other, more insistent noises soon alerted me.

A male voice, a hissed whisper: 'God—I've been waiting for that.'

And a female: 'You've no idea. Sitting there all day. Wanting to touch you.'

Various odd sound effects followed; wet noises, muffled drowning noises.

'Yes, touch me there.'

'You like?'

'Please.'

A violent movement rocked the shelves momentarily, and ejected a book onto the floor next to me with a thud.

I held my breath, listening to the sound of two people listening. And then the noise of sexual passion resuming, unstoppable.

'Give me it.'

'Here? Now?'

'Now! I'm going crazy . . .'

I knew what was happening, recognised these simple, stylised sentences from the movies. I bent—stealthily—and retrieved the book from the floor: *The Unconscious Beethoven.* About to slide it back into place I was halted, transfixed, by the view that presented itself through the narrow gap: a wet tongue nudging frantically at an ear, a pink fish trying to find its way back into some white, coral hole.

I bent a little lower and removed, silently, smoothly, the thickest book I could find: *Memoirs of Hector Berlioz.* The names of those books remain deeply branded in my memory, important not so much for what was in them as for what was *behind* them. I put my eye to the peephole.

A hand—a man's bristle-furred hand—could be seen kneading bare flesh.

'Kick them off,' the male voice commanded, mysteriously. 'And spread your legs.'

I dropped to my knees, and pressed my head flat to the floor. Peering beneath the bottom shelf I could just make out four feet: one pair shackled together by a pair of denim jeans around their ankles, the other pair in sandals, wider apart, a pair of panties lying some distance away . . . but wait, *how* many pairs of feet? Now only the male feet could be seen, straining in their denim shackles. The other pair had mysteriously levitated, even as I watched.

'That feels *so* good!'

'Much better when you have to wait for it.'

The shelves rocked gently again, and more books tumbled down. Still on my hands and knees, trembling with excitement and terror, I crept away down the aisle dog-fashion, an assortment of musicology texts raining down on me.

I remained on all fours until I reached the Mens', where in the secrecy of a locked cubicle I spent some time trying to fit together that jigsaw of oblong book-shaped peepholes into one whole thrilling picture: a picture I would take back to Darwin fixed in my repertoire of fantasies, ready for use when my own long-awaited First Time arrived, which was not—I desperately hoped—too far away . . .

In the car that night, on the way to a string quartet performance, my parents continued discussing the awful tragedy of Keller's life.

'And to think she was a Wagner specialist,' my father said. The irony had not escaped him.

'I can't believe,' my mother murmured, 'that a nation could murder so many of its musicians.'

'You think the murder of musicians is more serious than the murder of the tone-deaf?'

'Of course I didn't mean that. I meant what a *waste*, what a loss to the world, a squandering of all that training . . .'

As always, however, he was relentless: 'You mean: the more training you have, the worse the crime?'

'It just seems so terrible. We know the numbers of dead, the cold figures. But a particular story—a victim sang opera, a victim played the violin—makes it somehow more . . . real, able to be imagined. Like seeing those gold fillings in the newsreels.'

'The human angle. *I'm* more interested in the fact that she sang Wagner. I wonder if the poor woman ever sang for the Nazis—they *loved* Wagner.'

'It's all too horrible to talk about,' she said. 'All those millions of people.'

'As I understand it,' he pressed on. 'Some prominent Jewish musicians *were* protected. Some were made honorary Germans.

Hitler had his own list . . . First-rate Jews!'

I listened with half an ear only; interested yes, but far more interested in reliving other events from my day in the library.

1968

I returned to school in Darwin a year older and a year taller—
but I had not yet grasped the fact. Self-perception lagged
timidly behind my growth spurt: my body image refused to
grow. Looking down on my classmates, I still seemed to be
looking *up* at them. I walked round-shouldered, hunched, as
if trying to make myself smaller . . .

'Chest out,' my mother would urge. 'Don't slouch.'

'It's the piano,' I blamed.

And perhaps it was. Much of my life was spent hunched
over a keyboard. Even at school the Music Room was still
my lunchtime sanctuary . . .

From the beginning of that second year I often had company.
A new arrival from the South—Rosie Zollo, daughter of my
new French teacher—began creeping into the Music Room
each day to munch her sandwiches and listen to me play,
or ask questions about the beginner's pieces she herself
played.

'Looser,' I would counsel, repeating the clever phrases I
had learned from Keller. 'The hands must be looser. And
quicker. Like sprinkling salt.'

I suppose I disliked her for the usual reason: she was too
much like me. Also I was worried; I now had competition.
She was the other smart kid in the class. Her eyes would
fix on mine with a grim, suffering love throughout lunch. Her
voice seemed insistent, high-pitched, like an insect. I felt the
urge at times to swat the air near my ears, to drive that voice
away.

'I adore Mozart. It's like . . . sunlight, don't you think? A
dream of sunlight.'

My dreams—my sweet, sticky dreams, usually taking place
in a library, standing between shelves—were only of Megan.
And the fact that this intense, dark-haired girl worshipped
me? That only disqualified her even further. The old quandary:
anyone *that* desperate . . .

And yet I accepted her, even took pains to instruct her.
Some miserly part of me refused to give anything away, to
close off even the remote possibility of Rosie Zollo.

'Each finger has its own identity, Rosie. Take the thumb . . .'

I had no shortage of such advice: my repertoire was growing longer each lesson. It seemed that Keller was determined to punish me—or himself—for his excesses of Christmas gift-giving: lessons now lasted up to three hours, filled with scales, arpeggios, and the inevitable studies.

'Czerny without end,' he smiled grimly, always fond of attempting awkward puns in his second language.

And yet his attitude *had* changed, subtly. That Christmas card and priceless gift had opened a door, a narrow emotional chink. However gruffly he tried to slam it shut I was determined to keep my foot wedged in the crack.

'Tell me about Vienna.'

'Vienna was many places. And many times.'

'When you were my age. What was it like?'

'The Ballroom of Europe,' he said, mockingly.

'It must have been wonderful.'

He shrugged: 'I was busy.'

'But all the music. The famous musicians.'

'One day I looked up from my keyboard,' he said. 'And Vienna had gone. Finished. Become a wine garden filled with civil servants.'

I pursued the same theme for weeks, trying to draw him out.

'Gemütlichkeit,' he said.

'Sorry?'

'Versuchstation für die Weltuntergang,' he added.

I watched him blankly, waiting for a translation.

'The Experimental Laboratory for the End of the World,' he obliged.

I tried again, the following week: 'There must have been concerts. Theatre. So much to see and hear.'

'I sat in wine gardens and played skat,' he said. 'With civil servants. While the world ended.'

'But the beautiful opera houses. The concert halls. One day I'm going to play in those halls . . .'

'Perhaps,' he said. 'But who will listen? In Vienna the best

64

boxes face away from the stage, towards the rest of the audience. People come to watch each other, to be seen, not to listen. Vienna is the city of show, of . . . veneer.'

I was to be allowed no dreams, it seemed.

'You wish so much to know Wien? To understand those Great Times?'

I heard the bitter emphasis in his tone, but ignored it.

'Yes, I do.'

'Bring a pack of cards. I will teach you the game of skat. You must be prepared for the end of the world.'

———— ♦ ————

*I*f Vienna remained a closed book, Keller seemed more willing to share other thoughts. What he read in his newspapers, for instance. I had burned with curiosity about these; now I was given ample opportunity to slake it.

49 Arrested at Carols by Candlelight Riot.

'It is a kind of music, no?' he said, reaching for his scissors.

'It's funny.'

'It *might* be funny if so much did not depend on it.'

A vast collection of these much-thumbed scrapbooks was squeezed into the bottom shelves in his room. Waiting for him—he often had doctors' appointments during the first months of that year, and sometimes even seemed in pain, although he never mentioned it—I would sometimes leaf through the nearest book.

At times I would laugh out loud, at times I would avert my eyes in horror, unable to read further. There were clippings from days before and clippings dated back before my birth, all shades of newsprint from fresh, recent white back through various time-strata of faded grey and dirty yellow. Many were in German—*DIE ZEIT, DIE PRESSE* from Vienna—but the accompanying photographs looked much the same whatever the language, a bleak human landscape located somewhere between Tragedy and Dumb Stupidity. I guessed that the content of the German and English stories was much the same.

Many reminded me of the stories my father brought home from his work.

A medium, 53, no longer able to communicate with the dead after removal of a brain tumour, has successfully sued his neurosurgeon for malpractice. A Californian jury awarded the man $US 1.2 million damages for loss of paranormal powers.

'May I take this clipping home?' I said, wanting to show my father.

He watched me for a time, deciding: 'Take the whole textbook.'

'Scrapbook,' I corrected.

'You may return the textbook,' he insisted, meaning exactly what he said. 'Next week.'

I spent hours lying on my bed that night poring over the 'textbook'. LIBRETTO, he had scrawled violently across the front cover—some sort of fierce personal joke, obviously.

After listening to the evening radio concert, my parents joined me in my bedroom, curious to know what could produce such hoots of laughter, honks of disbelief. I could still hear them reading selected fragments aloud to each other as I lay in bed, at midnight, their voices amused and worried, carrying along the outside of the house:

His sole personal effects were a copy of Nietzsche's Twilight of the Gods, and a set of stainless steel false teeth.

I was forbidden access to the book on subsequent nights. Unsuitable, my father decided. Biassed. Out of Context.

'Out of bounds,' he warned, placing the scrapbook on a high shelf, just as in infancy all kinds of fragile and exquisite valuables had been stored beyond my grasp.

I could have reached the shelf easily, of course—but some sort of symbolic taboo remained, a shortfall in psychological reach, and I left it alone.

The scrapbook was handed to me as I left for my lesson the following week. After turning the first corner, I slowed to a crawl, then stopped altogether, leafing through:

Compensation Shock. Bereaved parents lash out. 'How can money bring back our son? $40,000 is nowhere near enough. We expected twice as much.'

Keller removed the book from my grasp as I entered the room.

'Your father has written,' he said. 'He feels you should not have an education.'

'And you?'

He squeezed the bulging scrapbook back among its companion volumes, and smiled grimly:

'If only at your age I'd had such textbooks.'

I let this pass without comment. I was interested, yes— but no longer obsessively. If he wanted to waste his life clipping stories of stupidity and squalor from the newspapers, so be it. I had better things to do.

'The Mozart?' I suggested, slipping a sheet of music onto the stand.

———— ✦ ————

The Wet was ending, the frogs outside my bedroom window croaking ever more loudly each evening in their shrinking creek, for diminishing returns. Fruit was suddenly everywhere: in snackbars, roadside stalls, gardens. My father couldn't pass a shop without stopping to buy smooth-skinned pawpaws, rough, soft avocados, a dozen crinkled passionfruit . . .

He had begun planting our own garden with seedlings and treelings: banana, custard apple, mango, babaco—and his prize possession, a single precious cutting of the legendary rambutan, a gift flown in illegally by one of his patients from Timor.

'The world's most delicious food,' he assured us.

'We'll have to take your word for that,' my mother teased.

'Only till the first crop.'

He was experimenting, he elaborated. Even perhaps planning to buy a few acres south of the town, and try something commercial. In the near future.

Medicine increasingly bored him. He felt burnt out, needed to recharge the emotional reservoirs. Each evening he sat over his evening meal imagining some hilltop dream plantation:

sprawling verandahs, rattan blinds, musical evenings amid the tropical fruit.

'Mangoes and Mozart,' he joked. 'Now *that's* living.'

'Mangoes and fruit bats,' my mother cautioned.

'Bananas and Bach.'

'Bananas and bankruptcy.'

He could smell Asia in the north-west monsoon, he liked to claim. The Spice Islands, three hundred miles away. Fecund, orchid spangled jungles. Rare, exquisite fruits. Fishing villages . . .

'I feel I've come home,' he said. 'Finally. I felt it instantly, that first night we stepped off the plane. The heat, the Wet— like a blanket.'

'Instantly? Seems to me you fought it.'

He smiled: 'Not for long. I've realised we're part of Asia here. Not Europe. We're Asians.'

'You don't look Asian.'

'We are what we eat. I'll buy you a wok.'

'A what?'

'A wok.'

'What on earth is a wok?'

'I don't know. But you need one. And some books. Malay cooking, Thai. *That* is what we should be eating—not grills and cold-climate vegetables.'

The Friday-night soirées continued that year, usually amid heaped bowls of tropical fruit, and in the lingering, saturating aroma of my mother's latest attempt at fish sambal, or stir-fry chicken and chillies and ginger.

A sub-committee had been formed with the purpose of flying concert artists up from the Southern cities. That Christmas in the South, during which my parents had attended every concert they could squeeze in, had whetted their appetites, made them remember the one thing missing from their life in Darwin. With the end of the Wet they scored a major coup: a visit from the Brisbane Symphony.

The town gentry were out in full that day, filling the natural amphitheatre in the Botanical Gardens: itinerant professionals from the South mostly—teachers and doctors, lawyers and civil servants—plus the odd local car dealer or furniture magnate or fruit-shop owner.

The rains were newly ceased, the sky washed clean and transparent. Cicadas roared in the trees, the gardens spilled over with colour and scent: frangipani, bougainvillea, hibiscus, poinciana. I sat with my parents on the terraced, grassy slope, trying to maintain some distance between myself and Rosie Zollo, who had abandoned her own parents to plop down at my side.

'You told me you weren't coming,' she teased, playfully, attempting to introduce a private bantering tone between us.

'Changed my mind,' I squeezed from one corner of my mouth, gazing fixedly in the other direction.

My mother leant across me, mistaking my sullenness for shyness:

'Perhaps you could introduce us to your friend, Paul.'

'Rosemary,' Rosie smiled. 'It's so nice to meet you, Mrs Crabbe.'

'That's a lovely frock you're wearing, Rosemary—isn't it Paul?'

But I had spotted Keller, shuffling into the gardens among the late stragglers, his white panama and glowing red face unmistakable.

'Look.'

My father half rose to his feet, waving a programme:

'Won't you join us, maestro.'

Keller doffed his hat, clambered with some difficulty up the steps and seated himself beside us. He did not look well. His hands trembled, and he clutched tightly at the brim of his hat as if trying to suppress that trembling. The sun beat down on him fiercely, magnifying all blemishes: the terracotta redness of his face, the deep fissures and cracks that gave his skin the texture of crudely fired pottery. I guessed he'd been drinking heavily—a hunch confirmed by the eloquent nose-wrinkle my mother gave my father behind his back.

'This is Paul's friend from school,' she smiled. 'Rosemary—this is Herr Keller, Paul's piano teacher.'

Rosie gushed: 'Paul's told me so much . . .'

Keller inclined his head slightly then returned his gaze to the soundshell. The orchestra, clad in white summer suits, was assembling. For the first—and probably last—time, his own formal tropical costume did not look out of place.

As the musicians finetuned their tools of trade, Rosie moved closer, squeezed against me by latecomers. Her thigh pressed suddenly against mine, and against my will I felt my pulse lurch and change tempo, accelerando.

I glanced at her, and found a miracle had occurred before my eyes. Or perhaps *after* my eyes, the miracle taking place somewhere between eyeball and brain. The mousy hair, usually held in prim school plaits, looked suddenly thick and lush. The nose—a bony wafer—was now almost dainty; the podgy baby-fat had become feminine softness. I watched— hypnotised—the slow, tidal rise and fall of her breasts with each breath.

My heart hammered inside me. I slipped an arm behind her, and she leaned slightly into me. Her perfume seemed an all-consuming sexual solvent . . .

Somewhere else the concert was beginning: Prokofiev, Peter and the Wolf, a children's classic.

'They've got Darwin's mental age worked out,' I breathed in Rosie's ear, feeling carnal, arrogant, invulnerable.

Various predictable favourites followed: the Jamaican Rumba, a Tchaikovsky Waltz, a couple of De Sousa marches. Each offering except the Tchaikovsky was rewarded with thunderous applause. The Tchaikovsky was followed first by a sort of communal sighing noise, a vast collective aah: the sound that I imagined the thirsty might make after a first long quenching. Especially the sentimental thirsty.

Rosie and I spent the Intermission pressing arms and thighs, trembling with excitement while appearing to remain still. The reckless confidence of lust had taken hold of me: I squeezed my hand along the grass beneath her, and held my breath, disbelieving, as she shifted herself on top of it. Somewhere in the background I could hear my parents attempting small talk with Keller, a task rendered even more difficult than usual due to his drunken state.

'You are enjoying the concert, Herr Keller?'

'The Prokofiev has a certain innocent charm.'

'I love Tchaikovsky myself.'

'My condolences, dear lady.'

After Intermission came a Mozart Piano Concerto, the C Major. A smattering of applause broke out in the audience after the first movement, and I shook my head and laughed harshly, manfully, at such ignorance.

'The plebs think it's finished,' I sneered to Rosie, who halted her own cupped hands, mid-clap.

No so Keller. *He* leant forwards into my field of view and began to deliberately strike his hands together, maintaining the noise, solo, long after the rest of the audience had stopped, and the conductor was waiting, white baton poised, to resume.

'We are *meant* to clap between movements,' he told me.

He rose to his feet, braced his shoulders, and sat again: 'And stretch our legs. It is you who are ignorant.'

His public rebuke infuriated me. I had been dragged to concerts in the South as soon as I could walk. I knew the correct procedure: proper concert-going etiquette. I took pride in knowing when a piece of music had finished.

Not even the second movement, the famous Andante, could soothe me. I soon decided it was being played very badly. This time Keller seemed in agreement: he withheld his applause after it, and again after the Allegro which followed.

'Wasn't that beautiful,' my mother murmured, as the soloist took a third bow.

'No,' Keller said, simply.

Wagner completed the programme: the Act 1 Prelude from *Lohengrin*. I can't listen to the piece now without seeing again the strange events that followed: a scene that seems to grow clearer in my mind the further I recede from it, like a slowly developing polaroid print, gaining colour and texture and detail even as I watch. Things I hadn't thought I'd noticed—too immersed in Rosie perhaps—have only surfaced since. Now I see it perfectly clearly: as the first bars of the Wagner shimmered into the air, and vanished, shimmered again and vanished again, Keller became very silent. Of course he would have been silent anyway, listening to the music, but *this* silence was somehow different, deeper, stronger: a zone of silence in the noise of the music, so deep that it . . . screamed.

The muscles of his face had frozen, his eyes were unblinking.

And suddenly he was wobbling to his feet, shouting in German.

A swirl of shushes washed against him from all sides, but he wouldn't be stopped. Neither would the orchestra: the conductor half-turned at the first interruption, and a few prim faces and glinting spectacles turned upwards from their instruments momentarily, but the music continued.

Tears were filling the deep fissures of that parched landscape, Keller's face. Weeping in his white tropical suit, he stood in the audience like a stranded member of the orchestra, unable to reach the stage, or not allowed to play.

Two ushers—volunteers from the Musical Society, well-meaning, dithering—were at his side:

'Please, maestro. Not again.'

Not *again*? The word stuck in my ear, and stayed there, trapped, buzzing.

'If you don't wish to listen, perhaps you could leave.'

He shrugged the various guiding hands from his elbows and moved slowly off up the grassy slope, alone. As suddenly as they had appeared, the tears had gone, sucked into the dry skin of his ravaged face.

'Bah!' he muttered—exactly like that, the only time I have heard the exclamation spoken as it is so often written: 'Bah!'.

My parents could talk about nothing else afterwards—an upper-case Scene—but I had other things on my mind.

'I'll just walk Rosie home,' I excused myself.

'Don't be late,' my mother smiled knowingly, meaning, I suspected, exactly the opposite.

The two of us wandered slowly, with a kind of aimless, accidental resolution, towards the thickest, darkest regions of the Gardens. In a small hollow among fig tree roots and ropes of lantana we managed to find some joint excuse to sit down, and then a further stammered excuse to lie down alongside each other.

But that was the end of stammering. We spent the rest of the afternoon in an agony of touchings and pleasures, fired by the kind of passion and inventiveness that only two frustrated loners were capable of, choreographing every sensual pleasure imaginable as if we had been dreaming of and planning for that moment for years.

——— ◆ ———

*F*or the first time as I climbed the wooden steps at the *Swan* that following Tuesday I heard the sound of a piano: music was being played on the *Bösendorfer*, the supine; and it was the kind of music that made me stand and listen outside the door, disbelieving. Keller playing *for himself*? And even— for now his voice came to me—*singing*?

I knew the piece well; Wagner again. My father often played orchestral excerpts from *Tristan* on his gramophone. But I had never heard it played quite like this: a piano transcription, accompanied by snorts of contemptuous laughter, and phrases of angry, broken singing.

There was passion in the voice, yes, but under immense pressure: a passion that was given in hints, then snatched away, given again, and disallowed again. It was an impossible, contradictory duet, or not so much a duet as a duel: a debate between two instruments, voice and piano. Or perhaps, more accurately, between head and heart. Contempt and self-hatred fuelled the singing of the voice, and all the while the hands played, autonomously, with an abandon and rapture beyond anything I had ever heard.

I stood transfixed at the door, overwhelmed, goose bumps rising, the hair on my neck standing on end. When he had finished, I waited some time before knocking tentatively.

'No lesson today,' he called gruffly through the door.

'But . . .'

'Practise your Mozart.'

I shifted feet for another minute or so, then knocked again. 'Are you alright?'

The door opened and he was revealed, his white suit crumpled and slept-in. But the eyes were clear.

'You are a good boy,' he said. 'Of course you must come in.'

The room was in darkness: the slats of the wooden louvres tightly shut, the lights off. A white blur of unmade bedsheets in one corner caught my eye, and light from the open door glinted here and there, reflected from various bottles on the floor.

No music stood on the grand piano. I realised he had been playing from memory. Or even—it would not have been past him—improvising.

'You have been listening?'

'It was wonderful. Magnificent.'

'No,' he said. 'It was interesting. Cheap tricks,' he continued. 'The interest here is technical only. How Liszt manages to transcribe Wagner's orchestral colour onto a piano.'

'But it's brilliant. It reaches in and . . . *lifts* you.'

'An intellectual exercise only. Listen—here are the first violins . . .'

He resumed playing, and with the first chords I was transported again to that same sensual, aching zone. The music seemed nearer to lovemaking than to music . . . and now I knew about lovemaking. I looked across at him; the tortured, booze-ruined face. His eyes were fixed on his silver clamshell of family photographs: on the woman standing behind his younger self, her mouth open in song. Perhaps she had been singing Wagner as the photograph was taken.

He reached the final crescendo: a great washing ocean, rising and falling, rising and falling . . . then he stopped, abruptly.

'It doesn't quite work here, you agree?'

'Well . . .'

'The rubato,' he said. 'A problem, no?'

'No,' I said, bravely. 'It's perfect. The most beautiful music I've ever heard.'

He turned sharply: 'Then we must continue your education. You cannot have heard much.'

I smiled, but internally, unseen, using no visible facial muscles. I was increasingly impervious to his criticism. I knew *my* kind of music when I heard it. The world of the mind was slowly losing its hold on me; the world of the senses replacing it. Each day my eyes seemed to be opened just a little wider, and more of that sun-drenched town of lush gardens, scents, and sexuality seemed to cram itself in. Nothing I heard in that dark, humid room in the *Swan* had much place in my new world—except perhaps the music I had just heard.

I wondered how I could get my hands on a copy of the transcription, and play it one lunchtime for Rosie.

——— ◆ ———

'**O**kay, lovebirds—out. You're trespassing.'
'But we practise here every day,' Rosie protested.
The door to the Music Room had flipped open, mid-lunch, and half the school pushed in, Scotty Mitchell at the head of the crowd, clutching an electric guitar.

'Practise what?' he asked, and his entourage chortled.

'You heard,' Jimmy Papas, standing at his shoulder, jerked a thumb towards the door. 'Out.'

Megan, her blonde cumulus of hair visible somewhere back in the crowd, intervened:

'The band needs somewhere to practise, Paul. You can't have the Music Room to yourselves *every* day.'

Scotty was already plugging his guitar into some sort of black box. Papas closed the lid of the piano I was playing, just slowly enough to allow me to extract my fingers without serious injury.

Rosie and I sat pressed together on the stool. I didn't want to move. The bulge in my shorts that she had been fondling as I played would surely cause even more laughter among the new arrivals.

'Can we listen?' I asked.

Outnumbered, outmuscled, we sat waiting for an answer which didn't come. Various strange string instruments were connected together, knobs fiddled, and the first few bars of amplified noise strummed.

There appeared to be three in the band—guitar, bass guitar, drums. The boys I knew only too well: Scotty Mitchell, Reggie Lim, and the notorious Jimmy Papas.

Papas was a central figure in my fantasy life: since that afternoon when he had waited for me in the bike shed I had spent many sleepless nights planning revenge. I was not alone. All over Darwin the slightly built, the bespectacled, the swots and the Sunday School students would lie in their beds at night, planning revenge on short, squat Jimmy Papas. Bennie Reid especially was full of wonderful schemes. Most recently— he boasted publicly, recklessly—he planned to wrap a fresh dogshit in newspaper, set it alight on Jimmy's doorstep, ring the bell and watch from safety as Jimmy stamped out the flames.

My own plan was simpler: I wanted only to bury Papas to the neck in the tidal flats, kick him very hard in the head a few times—nothing extreme, just breaking the nose and front teeth—then leave him to the incoming tide.

At the same time I often made a token effort to understand his thinking processes, to try to get *inside* him. Cruelty as a form of revenge, I could understand—this, in fact I planned myself. Likewise cruelty inflicted out of jealousy, or spite, or hatred—these implied a certain respect for, or fear of, the victim. But cruelty fuelled by no emotion at all? Bullying for kicks, arbitrarily dispensed, nothing more than a way of filling in time, a form of impromptu entertainment making use of whatever materials were at hand?

That was Jimmy Papas.

'Fuck off, Crabbe,' he advised. 'Real quick.'

'I have to pack my music.'

'Leave him, Jimmy,' Scotty Mitchell said. 'Let him hear some *real* music.'

Mitchell was taller, curly haired and good-looking in a squashed-nose sort of way. The local Golden Gloves champion, he would not have liked being labelled a bully. He used his fists just as freely around the school, but his self-image differed from Jimmy's. Scotty believed in Just Causes—however unjust they appeared to others. Not so much Protecting the Weak, for instance, as Sticking Up For A Mate. If he beat up someone half his size, it was not for pleasure but reluctantly, necessarily, to teach his victim a lesson. Perhaps even to make a man of him.

The third member of the trio was Reggie Lim: Chinese, diluted slightly with Aboriginal. Dark-skinned, his flat face pocked with the craters of largely extinct acne, Reggie looked fiercer than he was—a follower, not a leader.

Greek, Chinese-Aboriginal, Australian: the band might have been a statistical paradigm of Darwin's population, a band put together according to principles of affirmative action and proportional representation. In fact it was put together according to the principles of three young delinquents wanting to make a million bucks, or make a very loud noise, or some mix of the two.

I listened—packing my music, slowly—as they began picking a difficult path through a basic twelve-bar blues, trying to get by on three simple chords. Restricted in volume—part of the deal struck with school authorities—they were not even able to hide their clumsiness behind a wall of white noise.

'It's a matter of doing the simple things well,' I couldn't resist chiming in.

'You still here?' Jimmy Papas growled.

I lifted the piano lid and walked a simple bass riff down into the underworld regions and up again.

'You play rock'n roll?' Scotty wanted to know.

'I play everything,' I lied, never having played it before.

'So play,' Jimmy invited—or perhaps threatened.

I added the same few chords that they had been playing, staccato, in the right hand: C, F, C; G, F, C.

'Can you play this?'

Scotty passed over a sheet of music, something called *Hound Dog*, scored as simply as any Second Grade piano piece: melodic line and bass, with chord changes written above the staff every few bars.

Rosie moved sideways on the stool, and I played: once

through slowly to get the feel, then second time through camping it up, plenty of foot-stomping and keyboard-raking glissandi and shake, rattle and roll.

'Not bad,' Scotty admitted, reluctantly.

'Why don't we sound like that?' Reggie—catching the prevailing mood of tolerance—wanted to know.

'You weren't in tune,' I suggested, still uncertain how far I could push my luck. 'For one thing.'

Jimmy scowled: 'You got a guitar?'

'I've got an ear.'

Rosie snickered beside me. Even Megan was smiling, sitting on the floor against a wall in the background, her knees tucked under her chin. Remembering that moment, those brave words, I realise now they were a turning point: a fork in the path of my life, a spinning of the bottle that could have gone any way . . .

'What's the bottom string on one of those things?' I asked Scotty.

'E.'

'Okay—here's an E. Let's hear yours . . . no, too low. Higher. Still higher . . . You too, Jimmy.'

Finetunings completed—after some considerable time—I continued:

'Now a chord: C major chord.'

Scotty's left hand curled around his fret-board, slowly, clumsily seeking the right combination.

'Look,' I said, more and more in control, confidence climbing. 'I know a bit about music. Why not let me join you for a few sessions?'

Glances were exchanged among the three of them, a quick poll taken by nod or shrug.

'Nothing to lose,' Scotty tallied the votes.

'What the hell,' Reggie echoed, as always.

'What I'm going to say,' I said, 'might sound crazy. But stick with me. We don't play today. We begin with the basics: with the hands . . .'

I unclasped Jimmy's left hand from the bass guitar and held it in mine.

'If you wanted to hold hands, Crabbe,' he said, 'all you had to do was ask.'

Stump-fingered, broken-nailed, wire-fuzzed, that hand resembled more the club it often was than anything capable of producing music. But Keller's delicately podgy hands had taught me the shallowness of such judgements. And besides, I was enjoying the role: the private revenge of taming this wild animal, holding his lame paw, reciting to him a musical version of *This little pig went to market* . . .

'First the forefinger,' I began, almost wishing I had a pince-nez. 'He is our best pupil . . .'

Rosie snickered again, but Jimmy's uncurled fist lay dead in my palm, as if anaesthetised. A miracle was occurring. In the span of one lunchtime, music, the universal common language, would come to provide me with permanent protection in the schoolyard, and a safe conduct pass into even the darkest corners of the Covered Area.

——— ♦ ———

'*D*o you still dream of me?'
'Sometimes,' I lied.

Megan was driving her mother's car—the ink on her licence still wet, I suspected. We were heading in the wrong direction: past Scotty's house, our supposed destination, where the band was practising that night, and out along the East Point Road.

'We're early,' she said. 'Let's drive.'

It soon became clear that driving was not her intention: she halted the car in the shadow of the first gun emplacement, and turned towards me.

'Tell me.'

'Tell you what?'

'About the dreams.'

'I can never remember dreams,' I repeated the standard excuse, uneasily.

She moved closer, pushed her hand inside my shirt, and ran her fingertips over my bony chest:

'You've filled out, Paul.'

I was still beanstalk-thin, the skin wrapped like tent-canvas across my cage of ribs. Perhaps she was trying to persuade herself, to excite herself in some way. I made myself play the role, reaching over and rubbing gently at her breasts with the back of my hand:

'So have you.'

She laughed: always a stunning sight, that familiar piano lid, lifted. The sight and sound of that laugh reached into me and turned some deep tap: my pulse stumbled, blood lurched and changed course inside me.

'Would you like to get in the back?' she suggested.

'I'd rather stay here in the front with you,' I replied, and burst into nervous laughter at the old joke.

We sat watching each other.

'There's a rug in the back,' she said at length. 'Let's go for a walk.'

I threw the rug across my shoulder, and followed her into the nearest bunker. The sun was low over the harbour, the late afternoon light leaving the world gilded, flushed, dusty. Inside, in the warm half-darkness, she spread the rug on the sand, and draped herself across it.

'Peel me a grape,' she smiled.

It was a disappointment, at least for me. She was too selfish, I realised later. Too used to being desired, to never having to involve herself in any real way. As soon as I touched her she became floppy, inert, like something wanting to be kneaded. She loved to be touched, bitten, licked—but passively, as if on a pedestal, receiving some sort of sexual tithe.

'You're very good,' she murmured afterwards. 'I knew you'd be good.'

I snorted: 'How did you know?'

'You can tell.'

'*How* can you tell?'

'It's in the eyes.'

She laughed, teasing, but I was too worried to be seduced a second time.

'What if Scotty finds out?'

'I'm not about to tell him. Are you?'

'Are you joking?'

She stroked the bones of my chest again. I looked at her—the thick cloud of hair, the cheekbones, the eyes, the smooth, soft body I had dreamed of so often—and remained unmoved. The sum of all that beauty was somehow less than its parts.

'You want to do it again?' she said, meaning here, now.

'No,' I said, meaning forever.

We folded the rug, dusted ourselves free of sand, and drove back slowly towards Scotty's—then on past his house once again.

'Drop me at home,' I said. 'Tell the boys I'm crook.'

We drove on in silence.

'It was too wonderful,' I lied, as I climbed from the car. 'I couldn't concentrate on the band tonight.'

'Tomorrow night?' she said through the window.

'I've got a piano lesson.'

I watched till she had turned the corner, then climbed onto my bike and pedalled to Rosie's house. I wasn't so much guilty, I was terrified. Terrified that I might lose her.

Rosie was studying in her makeshift bedroom: a caravan dry-docked on bricks beside the house. Her parents were entrenched inside the house in the living room, listening to the radio.

'Paul?'

I pushed through the wire door, and sat on the tiny bench opposite her.

'I wanted to tell you,' I blurted out. 'I love you very much. There will never be anyone else.'

This was true—at least from *that* moment, and has been true ever since. She rose and sat herself on my knees, pressing her head hard against mine.

'I can't bear to be apart from you,' she said. 'I can't think of anything else.'

She moved her legs apart, and sat straddling me, face to face. Like me, she had no doubt rehearsed these movements many times in her head beforehand: her passion, her inventiveness only gave the impression of spontaneity. But our act was so good we even fooled ourselves. And after such beginnings, such primings of the sexual pump, anything was possible.

'You're all sticky,' she said, fondling. 'And gritty.'

'Sweat,' I improvised. 'I pedalled flat out. And I was at the beach earlier.'

I could hardly see her: my head congested with love, or lust, my eyes filming over. She wrapped her podgy, dimpled legs behind my back, and sitting there, facing each other, in that marooned, rocking caravan, her parents only a few feet next to us, we made slow, muffled, reckless love.

———— ♦ ————

Nothing seemed beyond me during those heady months: even spurning, however tactfully, any further rendezvous with Megan Murray. My body image had finally caught up with its physical envelope; had perhaps, in the case of my head, even swollen beyond it. I felt high, happy, invulnerable . . .

My parents were concerned: their son the serious scholar had gone missing, somewhere between May and July. Final school exams were only months away, but each evening I spent with Rosie Zollo.

'She's a nice girl, Paul . . . but don't you think it's getting a bit serious? A case of too much, too soon?'

'We study together,' I reassured them.

This was true, in part. We studied episodically, fitfully, when sensually exhausted. Perhaps we even learnt *more* that way, the odd scrap of knowledge pressed more deeply into our brains, imprinted by the sheer force of the emotions that filled us at the time.

'We trust your judgement, of course. But you have a whole life in front of you, both of you. Why not wait till *after* the exams?'

'We complement each other. I help her with maths, she helps me with French.'

I paused, then added: 'We help each other with Biology.'

That I could risk such a joke is a measure of my arrogance at the time. But my parents had other preoccupations: Gilbert and Sullivan rehearsals—*The Gondoliers*—took up much of their time, leaving me free, unsupervised. I had been excused from opera duties for the first time; study commitments in my final year were felt too pressing. And so my nightly meetings with Rosie continued: our study group of two. I spent each evening with her, and each weekend in band practice, or at the drive-in, or swimming at various waterholes, springs, beaches . . .

Transport was no longer a problem: Jimmy's new panel van had arrived from the South. A sixteenth-birthday gift from doting parents—wealthy beyond their means of commonsense—that panel van was the first of its kind to reach Darwin. I can still recite from memory the strange-sounding Poem of Parts: Mags, Fats, Side-spoilers, Bubble Windows . . .

It resembled nothing so much as a giant bush fly: crouched low and road-hugging at the front, jacked up over absurdly wide tyres at the back, its panels spray painted iridescent glitter-blue.

Inside a kind of Pop Surrealism prevailed: tasselled curtains, sheepskin seat covers, panther pink carpet on the dash, a tiny plastic skeleton dangling and twitching from the rear-vision mirror.

DON'T LAUGH—YOUR DAUGHTER MAY BE IN HERE proclaimed a sticker on the rear-window.

Jimmy was full of himself: leaving thick black texta trails of tyre rubber around town, and swaggering about school, being an even bigger hero to all his various smaller apprentice bullies. I was lucky to be counted Friend.

Others were not so fortunate, Bennie Reid most frequently among them. Jimmy had appointed himself Official Protector of Butterflies.

'Still murdering butterflies, Reid?'

'Let go. You're *hurting* me.'

'Why don't you stick your little pins in something your own size?'

'They only live a few days anyway, you greasy wop. What can it matter?'

Bennie had decided to do it the hard way. Perhaps he had nothing to lose; certainly no known survival strategy—apology, flattery, even keeping out of Jimmy's way—made any difference. The pain he suffered was terrible, yes—but pain always passed, and when it passed anger still remained.

'Is it true you shave the palms of your hands, apeman?'

If he *had* to suffer, he might as well score points. He might as well go down fighting, even if only with a sharply stropped tongue:

'You could lend the razor to your mother afterwards, wog.'

I had to admire Bennie's courage, or his stupidity.

'Leave him alone, Jimmy,' I tried to defuse things. 'He's not worth it.'

'Did you hear what he *called* me?'

There was no standing between them. The victim also refused to allow it:

'You didn't hear what I called him? I'd better say it again. He's a wog. And you're a . . . a greasy crawler.'

Jimmy had met nothing like it. His victim would limp away in tears, and still turn and throw some last outrageous provocation back across his shoulder. Or brood for days, carefully planning more elaborate revenge.

'Smoke was coming out of the van,' Jimmy explained, angrily. 'There was this ball of newspaper burning on the floor under the dash. I stamped it out . . .'

'It was full of dogshit?'

'How did *you* know?'

'Bennie Reid.' The name slipped from my mouth, and could not be returned there for safekeeping, no matter how much I regretted it.

'*Reid!* I knew it!'

I visited Bennie that night to warn him. His parents were out, and he spoke to me through the locked flyscreen door, without letting me in. A tubby, middle-aged man, aged sixteen.

'I knew you'd tell him,' he said. 'You're that sort of person.'

I stood at the top of the steps outside his door, in a bright cone of light. A cloud of moths battered themselves against me.

'It just slipped out,' I said, swatting. 'I didn't mean . . .'

'You don't understand, do you Paul? I *wanted* you to tell him. I wanted him to know who did it.'

'He's going to kill you.'

He shrugged behind his flyscreen:

'It's not over yet: the dogshit is just the beginning. But don't let me keep you from your friends . . .'

'They're *not* my friends. It's just . . .'

He slammed the door in my face, and I was left with no-one to convince except myself: a much easier task, I found as I walked slowly home, than trying to convince him.

I squirm now remembering my part in this. At the time those excuses seemed entirely reasonable. I couldn't stop Jimmy— but perhaps I could dilute his rage. And Bennie's harsh words? Nothing could dent my invulnerability.

Not even the weekly consultation with Keller at the *Swan* could subdue me. Reckless with self-confidence, growing ever fonder of the sound of my own voice, I began squeezing him harder for information. For the first time I felt strong, or callous, enough to raise the subject of his wife, to follow the lead of that footnote I had found buried in an Adelaide library the previous summer.

'Your wife was Jewish, maestro?'

'My wife had little interest in religion.'

'But she had Jewish ancestry?'

'Is this important? If not, play the Mozart again.'

I played for a time before continuing, asking the question I had wanted to ask for months:

'I don't understand why didn't you leave.'

'Leave where?'

'Vienna. When the Nazis took over. Weren't you worried?'

'We always hope for the best. These things are always more simple to decide in retrospect.'

'But many Jews *did* leave. Why didn't you?'

He glared at me:

'Perhaps for the same reason you ask such a question,' he said.

'What's that?'

'I was too insensitive.'

———— ◆ ————

I sat beneath the house of Scotty's absent parents, pretending to enjoy my first beer. I felt immensely content: the sun was shining, the sky was blue, my new friends surrounded me. Rosie lay on her belly at my feet, scribbling simplified arrangements of the latest hits, trying to find the lowest common musical denominator, some crude level at which all the members of the band could participate.

Rehearsals were now fully portable, piano movers no longer required: two appearances at school fetes, one School Dance, and a street performance at the Darwin Mardi Gras had brought in enough funds for a cheap keyboard organ and amplifier.

I was beginning to feel more ambitious: the annual Battle of the Sounds was approaching, and anything was possible.

'What's first prize?' Scotty, sprawled on his back, naked from the waist, asked.

'A trip South for all of us,' I told him. 'And a place in the Adelaide final.'

'And if we win that?'

'Money,' I promised. 'Fame. Beautiful groupies.'

'Forget the money and fame,' he laughed.

Megan, smocked amidst tubes of paint, and pots of brushes, was stencilling the band's newly elected name—*Rough Stuff*—onto the membrane of the bass drum. She turned, feigning anger:

'You want me to do this or not?'

Rosie echoed her: 'If you're not careful you'll lose the only two groupies you've *got*.'

86

In a far corner, behind a low wall of empty beer bottles, Jimmy was going through the motions—largely pointless—of tuning his electric bass. He too had stripped to his waist. His body was covered with black fur, stiff as steel wool.

'We haven't a chance,' he said.

I was ready for doubts: 'Maybe not in Adelaide. But we can win here. We're the only rock'n roll band for a thousand miles.'

'This is the bush. Some country and western outfit always wins.'

'Not this year.'

'You know something we don't?'

I sipped at my beer, but only for show, allowing none to enter my mouth. I liked the idea of beer, but I loathed the actual taste.

'I know who the judge is.'

'Slim Dusty?' Reggie, an occasional comedian, put in.

I waited till the various snorts of amusement stopped: 'You might not believe it . . .'

'Save the suspense, Paul.'

'Trust me,' I smiled.

'Fucking *tell* us. Or I'll job you.'

'Rockin' Rick Whiteley. The Noise of the North himself.'

The boys were silenced, impressed. A newcomer from the South, Whiteley's Drive-Time Top 40 on the local radio was followed cultishly by every High School student. Various rumours held that he had fled North for various unspeakable reasons—that he had been tarred and feathered in several Southern cities. Whatever the truth, he seemed far too smooth, too sophisticated for the backwoods.

Butter-voiced, afro-haired, Whiteley put his life in jeopardy his very first time on Darwin air. Never again, he announced, would the country and western ballads of Slim Dusty get airplay while *he* was running things.

'Not even as a request,' he boasted. 'Not even as a *last* request.'

The Hate Mail flooded in, and was jauntily read aloud each day by Whiteley between the new, foreign sounds of Jimi

Hendrix and The Stones and The Doors. Letters from irate truckies, aboriginal stockmen, concerned Mothers of Six, Christians for Clean Airwaves . . .

The revolution lasted one week. Whiteley suddenly found himself on the graveyard shift, midnight to dawn, a punitive demotion which caused an after school sit-in of school students in the lobby of the radio station, the ringleaders being three of the four members of *Rough Stuff*.

The fourth member had a piano lesson.

A compromise was reached, amid much useful publicity: Whiteley agreed to permit one country and western track per hour if he was returned to afternoon radio. Even then, he refused to suffer in silence. That hourly token track soon became legendary.

'Is it the bushflies?' he would interrupt. 'The art in country music is to keep the mouth shut, and sing through the nose.'

He was always worth hearing on this one subject, a calculated Hate that was capable of lifting his standard disc-jockey patter into gusts of poetry.

'Send me your letters,' he would sneer. 'And I will tell you the angle of your ears to the side of your head.'

Or he would sing along, his normal syrup-patter stretched into a drawling, elastic monotony. Or the track would be followed by total silence—a horrified silence, we were given to understand.

'Water,' he would finally croak. 'Water . . .'

'They'd never let Whiteley near a judging panel,' Scotty was certain. 'The station has been trying to get rid of him since he arrived.'

I flourished a leaf of paper: 'One Official Entry Form to the Northern Territory Battle of the Sounds, bearing the name of the sole adjudicator. With whom no correspondence may be entered into . . .'

The boys crowded about, bending awkwardly over their guitars.

'He must have *bought* the station,' Jimmy declared.

'That's his problem,' I said. 'Ours is this: what do we play on the big night?'

'He'd give us first prize for *Jingle Bells*,' Scotty said. 'He owes us. Did we tell you about the sit-in? Went back to his place afterwards. Got drunk.'

'Whiteley was wandering around in his jocks,' Jimmy put in. 'Wanted us to tell dirty stories all night. Then he got weepy . . .'

'He's weird,' Scotty said. 'Can't hold his booze. Wanted to know if we'd ever been *Boy Scouts* for fuck's sake! I almost decked him. But he's got some great Chuck Berry tapes.'

'Then we play Chuck Berry,' I decided. 'Whoever Chuck Berry is.'

Scotty shook his head in disbelief: 'For a famous rock star you are pig ignorant, Paul.'

'So educate me.'

'The King of Rhythm and Blues,' he said, quoting I guessed from some record jacket he'd once glimpsed. 'You must have heard his stuff. On Golden Oldies.'

'It's old stuff?'

'Ten years,' he guessed. '*Reelin' and Rockin'*. It's a *classic* for Christ's sake.'

Jimmy tried to be practical. 'Where are we going to get the music?'

'Just get me the discs,' I said. 'LPs, 45s—whatever. I'll write out the parts. All I need is a melody line.'

'Why not borrow Whiteley's tapes?' Jimmy suggested. 'Tell him we loved them so much we just *gotta* hear them again . . .'

'You've got the job,' I said, more and more at home in the role of decision-maker.

'Borrow a Boy Scout uniform,' Scotty added. 'But don't get too close to him. He spits all over you when he's talking.'

The Town Hall was packed on the Big Night. Special Effects had been installed, an approximation of the more sophisticated discotheque decor of the South: strobe lighting, revolving mirror-balls, projectors screening continuously on all four walls and ceiling, coloured lights.

But despite this, there remained something of a School Dance feel about it: something dated, amateurish, thrown together by a Volunteer Committee.

'Let's rock,' Rockin' Rick Whiteley yelled. 'Let's stomp the night away.'

As I had missed the sit-in this was my first glimpse of him. Small and animated, with a huge fuzz of hair, there was something cartoonish about him, something bouncy, big-eyed, disproportionate: as if he were an animal character with human traits. If certain of the rumours could be believed, he was in fact a human with animal traits.

'Very nice, boys,' he was telling our main opposition—a jazz combination from Alice Springs—amid a smattering of ritual applause. 'Very nice. It was so . . . well, nice.'

We waited side-stage, tough and smirking in leather jackets and mirror sunglasses as the older jazz players—their musical skills far beyond ours—filed past in beards, berets, duffel coats.

'And *now*, groovers . . . ,' the Noise was rhapsodising, trying to talk the occasion up into something greater than it was, ' . . . Darwin's very own rock'n roll band: *Rough Stuff*. Reggie Lim on drums. Let's hear if for Reggie . . . Jimmy Papas on bass. On lead—hit it Scotty Michell. And on keyboards . . . Paul Crabbe. Go, Paul . . . '

Did we have to play a single note to win? Probably not. Tuning our instruments on stage would have been enough to take first prize. But we played several notes, in various recurring combinations, and several chords, with a lot of backing noise. *Reelin' and Rockin', Sweet Little Sixteen, Rock'n Roll Music*—plus one compulsory 'original' track.

Original at any rate in the sense that a few minor melodic changes, a couple of bass riff surprises were enough to differentiate it from any other twelve bars of rock'n roll ever written, and place it fractionally beyond the reach of the laws of copyright.

Scotty supplied the lyrics: a poem constructed entirely of monosyllables, as if according to the strict rules of some new, difficult literary form:

You Gotta Give Me What I Ask You For,
That's The Way It's Gotta Be

You Gotta Give Me What I Ask You For
You Just Gotta Set Me Free.
You Gotta Give Me What I Ask You For
You'll Just Love It Just You See

'What a sound,' the Noise shouted into the din of applause. 'What a band! And what a song! Roll over Lennon and McCartney, here come Crabbe and Mitchell.'

I loved it at the time: the driving rhythms, the wall of noise, the carefully cued screams of Rosie and Megan and the rest of our schoolmates. But, afterwards, sitting there in the spotlight, I was unable to take it seriously. For one thing, the sheer *hurt* of the sound we produced always, absurdly, made me want to use my bowels. The deafening volume seemed to trigger some deep, physiological reflex. Even then I couldn't help seeing it in those terms: Music to Shit By.

More serious was another problem: at the post-competition party under Scotty's house, surrounded by well-wishers, the puritan in me began re-asserting itself. Had I done anything to deserve this fame, this brief moment on the dais?

I felt strangely empty, deflated. Nothing worthwhile was ever achieved so easily, a small voice—perhaps my father's, perhaps Keller's—nagged deeply inside. Rosie also—after all her screaming—seemed subdued. Scotty was upstairs in his bedroom with Megan; Jimmy had been backed into a corner by Rockin' Rick, who was plying him with Southern Comfort and trying to persuade him of the merits of having his biceps tattooed; Reggie was surrounded by a crowd of smaller Reggies, even the tiniest of which already seemed covered with acne.

I took Rosie's hand and we wandered down to the foreshore and along the beach. The party was soon beyond earshot. A thin nail-clipping moon floated high in a dark, empty sky; the only music was the soft hush and crash of the waves, half-silence.

'It's all a joke,' she said. 'But it's fun.'

Or perhaps she didn't say it, perhaps she only thought it. More and more words seemed unimportant between us; or those words at any rate which had to do with feelings. Like twins, we knew each other's hearts . . .

I still have the clipping from the next morning's paper: a yellowing photograph of three sweat-soaked, beaming musicians, front-stage, their healthy boyishness shining inescapably through their glistening leather jackets and glinting sunglasses and sweat-varnished faces.

SCHOOLBOY MUSICIANS OFF TO ADELAIDE, AIM FOR BIG TIME.

Behind them, half-hidden, the keyboard player can be seen, looking pale and confused and in some pain—wanting to shit, perhaps. And yet the sheer inappropriateness of the leather hung on *his* pale, skinny frame somehow lends an unhealthy, improvised, and—finally—authentic rock muso look.

A paradox: of the four, only he looks the part.

Adelaide

'*I* believe you will be travelling to Adelaide,' Keller murmured as I sat at the *Wertheim* the following Tuesday. 'In the near future.'

He made no mention of how he had heard the news. Nor did he pass judgement, but I imagined that if I examined closely the smudged white elbows of his linen suit I might have seen my face hidden there, and reversed as if in a mirror.

'I trust,' he continued, 'that you will have a pleasant holidaying.'

A wry smile twitched at the edge of his lips. Of course he had read that newspaper—he read everything. I wondered if the item had been sufficiently curious to snip out and paste . . . in his 'textbook'.

'Perhaps while you are holidaying you might kill two birds. The Conservatorium in Adelaide wrote to me some time ago. Your exam results last year . . .'

He rose and fossicked in a bunch of papers on top of his fridge, feigning indifference.

'Somewhere here. Ah, yes. There is a competition you might enter. If you have time while you are . . . holidaying.'

'A Piano Competition?'

'Of course.'

The smile balanced again at the edge of his lips, then tilted back inside.

'There is not much money involved. And it is unlikely that your photograph will appear in the paper.'

'Do *you* think I should play?'

He refused to be drawn:

'That is your decision. If you plan a career in music you must start making a name for yourself. People must feel comfortable with your name. Like a . . . familiar brand name.'

His gaze moved to the shelf above his small fridge: 'Bushells. Heinz. Kraft. Kelloggs . . .'

He read slowly, deliberately, mockingly: his accent rendering the familiar names strange and exotic.

'. . . Bismarck.' He finished the inventory with the brand name of his usual schnapps, and smiled to himself.

'Do *you* think I'm good enough?' I tried again.

Again he deflected the question. 'The standard will not be high.'

'I may as well play.' I tried to match his offhandedness. 'Since I'll be there anyway.'

'Then we will talk to your parents.'

The more thought I gave it, the more the idea grew on me: this extra excuse was exactly what I needed. My mother had not been overjoyed at the success of the band in the Battle of the Sounds, or the planned trip South.

'Where will you be staying?' she had wanted to know.

'The radio station pays for our hotel.'

'Unchaperoned?'

'Jimmy Papas is sixteen. Nearly seventeen. And the disc jockey might be coming—Rick Whiteley. He wants to manage us. We'll stick together. What can happen to us?'

'I'm more concerned over what might happen to Adelaide,' my father said. 'And this Whiteley fellow. I'm not sure he's suitable.'

'We hardly know the boys in your ensemble,' my mother added. 'Why haven't they been around more? Why do they always sit out on the fence, waiting? Why don't they come in?'

She insisted on calling *Rough Stuff* an ensemble. Never having heard us play, perhaps she imagined it was some sort of string quartet.

'They're my *friends*, Mother.'

Mother. Was this the first time I had used the word in that way—keeping her at a distance, as if with a verbal barge pole. Certainly somewhere in that year she had made the transition from Mum to Mother: the journey of nuances.

'Are they nice boys? That Jimmy Papas—I've heard he's a troublemaker. And Reggie Lim—the boy with the terrible acne . . .'

'He can't help his acne.'

'Thank God for his acne,' my father chimed in. 'It would make things much harder without it.'

'What do you mean?'

'I've been thinking about it. Acne serves a useful purpose. It helps render our children ugly to us. Makes the pain of final separation easier to bear. Imagine having to love Reggie Lim . . .'

'This is *serious*, John. We're talking about the company our son keeps.'

So the news of the piano competition, a Battle of much more respectable Sounds, changed her attitude in the space of a single evening, although the usual dialectic of jostling and shifting positions continued long after I was in bed.

'He *could* stay with your parents,' I heard my mother saying in the lounge.

'Are we giving too much importance to one competition in Adelaide? At this age? What about his schooling?'

'Herr Keller must think it important. Perhaps one of us could travel down with the boys. Keep them under supervision.'

'Impossible for me,' my father said. 'But I'll talk to Keller next Tuesday after the lesson. I can sneak out of the hospital early.'

Keller had also been giving the trip some thought. He began as soon as I was seated at the piano.

'I know how these judges think,' he said. 'They seek athletes, not musicians. They judge a scherzo with a stopwatch . . .'

He scrabbled through a heap of yellowing Chopin albums and finally set the B-Flat Minor Scherzo on the stand:

'We will go one better,' he smiled grimly. 'For them we *pretend* to be athletes. For ourselves, we play music—at the same time! We win the race, and we also keep our self-respect.'

He played the Chopin through from memory. Apart from the Wagner, I had seldom heard him play more than a few bars at a time, or the same phrase over and over again. Certainly I had never been allowed this: a complete performance, uninterrupted, that lifted me onto my feet, exulting, with the first fortissimo response to the bass murmur. I stood at his shoulder, shifting from foot to foot, overcome, bursting inside with song.

'Terrible,' he shook his head, finishing.

'Sounded fine to me.' I tried to remain nonchalant, understated.

I sensed immediately that he'd been practising. Perhaps only once or twice—he would have needed no more—but his apparently casual plucking of the Scherzo from a pile of sheet music, his feigned indifference in whether I entered the competition or not: these were suddenly revealed to me as a sham. He could lie through his teeth as much as he liked, but sooner or later his hands—his wonderful hands—would betray him.

Together we began to take the Scherzo apart, phrase by phrase.

'This part is *not* for the stopwatch. More a . . . slow bike race. Do you have them in this country? You must keep the note aloft without playing—the *memory* must linger through a silence longer than you can bear . . . and then more. You must keep the hands still, the bicycle balancing with nothing but nerve . . .'

Two hours must have passed in this fashion. Sometime during the second of them my father must have crept unnoticed into the room and sunk himself into the armchair.

'Enough of your solo piece,' Keller finally said. 'What of the concerto?'

This was news to me: 'I have to play a *concerto*?'

'Of course.'

'With an orchestra?'

'It is possible. But a second piano, more probably. Taking the orchestral part. And that is how we will practise.'

He began fossicking once more in his shelves.

'I have very little of this music. We will have to make do.'

Another clump of torn, yellowing pages was set before me: the piano part of the Beethoven G Major. My father half-rose from the armchair, peering at the score. Perhaps he wondered if it was another first edition.

'Let us dismantle,' Keller said.

And so began the most concentrated period of study I had ever experienced. We finished at midnight, my father periodically leaving us to phone my mother with progress reports, revised meal scheduling—and I suspected, to grab a beer and sandwich at the bar downstairs. I also was hungry—I had not eaten—but there was no informing Keller of such trifles.

'Tomorrow,' he finally said, closing his piano, 'we begin the second movement.'

My relief was brutally cut short. 'You want to see me tomorrow?'

'Of course. We must practise daily.'

How could I tell him that I planned a different sort of practice, that I needed to write out new chord changes and bass riffs for *Reelin' and Rockin'*? I could not even have told him that I needed to study for school exams: Differential Calculus and *Great Expectations* and Garibaldi's First Landing on Mainland Italy. All of this was, suddenly, nothing.

'Even so the boy will not be ready,' Keller was saying to my father. 'Do you still wish him to play?'

'It seems an opportunity . . .'

'Then I am forced to travel with him. We must practise till the last. Of course I will play the second piano in the competition. Otherwise we cannot guarantee the accompaniment. Most play this Beethoven far too slowly.'

'We couldn't ask . . .'

'It is necessary.'

The wall was still there—the pretence that my incompetence, or someone else's, was to blame for the fact that he must travel South with me. But I didn't for a moment believe him. Nor did my father. His eyes met mine as Keller muttered crustily to himself, and he winked.

'We appreciate the sacrifice,' he murmured, realising it was pointless to protest further. 'Perhaps we could help with something towards your costs. An air fare . . .'

'Impossible,' Keller snapped, his gruffness perhaps compensating for the glimpse he had allowed us of a more tender inner core. 'Of course I could not accept.'

This was another revelation, in a day of revelations. I had always believed—prompted perhaps by my parents joky references to his drinking habits—that Keller lived day-today, financially. Or bottle to bottle—dependent on each week's tuition fees to pay for the next glass of schnapps. His refusal of financial help now was the first clue that money was the least of his worries. And also a clue that his contempt for teaching music to me was just another charade. Clearly he didn't have to teach. His contempt was fuelled by feelings far more complicated and contradictory than I had thought.

The implications were obvious: his exile was chosen, not forced upon him. He had enough money to fly anywhere he pleased, to *live* anywhere he pleased.

But chose not to.

---◆---

Now I felt a Territorian's contempt for Adelaide and its neat rows of suburbs as we circled to land. A temperate zone city of grandparents and churches, I decided. Of rotary clothes hoists and rose beds and apricot trees and cream-brick Dream Homes. All the old wonder seemed to have vanished, the magical City of years past—the Capital City of the land of Childhood—had become just another city, lower-case. My contempt was no doubt far greater than any native Territorian would have felt: I was one of the converted, always the most zealous believers.

I was to board with my grandparents in their seaside suburb; Keller had taken lodgings at a nearby motel, within easy walking distance.

The rest of the band were following by panel van, slowly, their air tickets cashed in for extra spending money.

Each morning Keller arrived for breakfast, a little out of breath from the walk, but resplendent in white suit and panama hat, pince-nez and walking cane.

Grandmother Wallace was most taken with her Continental Gentleman and his gruffly formal manners. Breakfast was the only meal he shared with us, and she soon determined to make the most of it: to lift it beyond the realm of the daily and mundane. I could set from memory a replica of the perfect Still Life she laid out on the table each morning: the carefully folded *Advertiser*, the two canary yellow hemispheres of grapefruit in their bowls, separated by a more richly yellowed cube of butter; the sky blue milk-jug and matching sugar bowl filled to the brim with their differently textured whitenesses; the pot of tea snug in its knitted navy blue cosy, the steam that rose invisibly from its spout suddenly rendered visible, swirling, where it entered the slanting morning light.

Conversation over the breakfast table also belonged to a higher, mannered plane, as if brought forward from later, more formal mealtimes.

'Have you had the pleasure of hearing our orchestra, Mr Keller?'

'This is my first visit to Adelaide, Mrs Wallace.'

'You must miss having an orchestra in the North. Ours is highly regarded. When Mr Rubinstein was touring—some years ago—and played here he said . . .'

'Could you pass the newspaper, dear lady?'

Keller was always far more interested in the headlines than in the opinions of Mr Rubinstein.

'Have you heard Mr Rubinstein play, Mr Keller?'

'Once,' he murmured. The implication was one that only I could hear.

'He played the Tchaikovsky Piano Concerto,' she continued. Perhaps you know it?'

I didn't know where to look: 'Of *course* he knows the Tchaikovsky, Gran.'

'In fact I have seldom played it,' Keller said—with a careful politeness designed to be taken in two ways, as if speaking two different languages simultaneously—carrying a different message to each of us.

'It's a wonderful piece,' she decided to remind him. 'The opening chords especially.'

His red, corrugated face remained bent to the morning paper: COSMONAUT IN RECORD FLIGHT. BIZARRE MURDER—SUICIDE PACT.

'We used to subscribe, of course. To the orchestra. But

Wilfred gets so tired now. I believe a concert is scheduled this Saturday night . . .'

'Unfortunately I have a prior commitment, dear lady.'

Wilf—my grandfather—was not so easily impressed. After a few initial attempts at communication—offers of a beer, politely declined, attempted reminiscences of the War, tactfully deflected—he returned to his sleep-out bedroom, to which he had been banished from the master bedroom some years before, and in which he spent most of his days listening to horse races and reading detective fiction.

After breakfast we practised: a three-hour stretch. In that time the Concerto might be allowed one or two partial hearings. At first there was only one piano; a second had been hired, but not yet arrived. As I played, Keller sang the orchestral part. His hoarse, breaking voice, I decided, would be much better suited to the blues, or even Chuck Berry.

Occasionally he spent our morning 'consultation' playing himself: filling in the background, playing various contrasting snippets from other pieces, relating anecdotes from Beethoven's life, demonstrating the different techniques of interpretation used by different artists, even at times improvising amusing parodies of whatever phrase or harmony we were examining.

'Parody,' he liked to tell me, 'is a form of homage, yes. And a form of . . . immunisation. But also fun.'

Fun was not a word that emerged easily from that wrinkled prune-mouth. It seemed a grim sort of fun as he turned my precious Czerny studies upside down and hammered out the melodic line, backwards and inverted, accompanied by absurd harmonies. Like so many of his sarcastic verbal asides, there was something not so much amusing as tormented in all this.

At noon he would vanish, by taxi, returning shortly with a thick stack of newspapers. As I ate my lunch he would sit in the lounge, reading, limiting his own midday meal as always to coffee. But no schnapps. It was a sight I had often seen in Darwin, on the balcony of the *Swan*: Keller hunched over his papers, elbows propped on the table, pince-nez adhering somehow to his nose, his brow furrowed, his gaze frequently switching from paper to paper mid-column as though comparing different versions of the same story.

'I can see you are a kindred spirit,' my grandmother told him, scrabbling to find common interests, or some shared language. 'I can't seem to get started in the morning without my *Advertiser*.'

'I loathe all newspapers,' Keller assured her. 'The goitre of the world, a friend of mine once described them. But we must study the goitre, carefully. Like doctors. Pathologists.'

He read those newspapers as closely as Bible texts, as though some sort of answer, or final explanation, or even *cure* could be discerned there, given enough time.

'Anthropology,' he explained to my grandmother, a little less harshly. 'The proper study of mankind is man, to quote one of your English poets.'

She fussed about him, fetching fresh coffee, plying him with questions, steering the conversation onto safer grounds.

'Where do you have such lovely summer suits made, Mr Keller?'

'I am fortunate, dear lady, to have found a very fine Chinese tailor. In Darwin.'

'Very fine' was his highest compliment, his single superlative. The most praise my playing had ever received was 'fine', or more usually, 'adequate'.

After lunch, textual analysis of the newspapers completed, we returned to the keyboard, and a shorter, more disciplined session: two hours of studies and exercises, ending, in the late afternoon, with one unbroken performance, under 'concert conditions'.

Then he would leave, driving off alone by taxi to eat at some Hungarian restaurant he'd discovered, his white Panama dazzling above his red face, a white cane tucked beneath his arm.

'Spend time with your grandparents,' he would murmur, excusing himself. 'I am too much between you.'

———— ◆ ————

'Y ou wouldn't read about it, Paul! What we didn't get up to!'

Keller had left by taxi only seconds before—a near thing— as the panel van reversed into my grandparents' gravel drive. Jimmy Papas's black-bearded head craned from the driver's window, twisted backwards, beaming. The sun was setting, light leaching rapidly from the world, colours greying, fine detail blurring into shadow. But the van still glittered, green-blue, finding sufficient light somewhere, the centre as always of the visual world.

Scotty climbed from the passenger door, crumpling an empty beer can. He flipped up the hatch and began unloading the black boxes and cables of our musical life-support system.

'What are you doing?' I wanted to know.

'Can't practise at the hotel. They won't hear of it.'

'You want to practise *here*?'

'There's nowhere else.'

'But my grandparents . . .'

Somewhere inside the house two elderly innocents sat watching their favourite quiz show.

'Give them our rooms at the Grosvenor,' a voice suggested from inside the van. 'A second honeymoon while we practise here for the week.'

Then Rick Whiteley emerged, disengaging himself from a tangle of equipment and empty beer cans.

'Where's Reggie?' I asked.

'Rick's on drums this trip,' Scotty told me. 'Reggie couldn't make it.'

Suddenly no-one wanted to meet my eye.

'Whiteley's playing *drums*? With *Rough Stuff*?'

Whiteley stretched his small limbs, and brushed himself down. 'I get by,' he said. 'I hold my own on skins.'

'He's fantastic,' Jimmy added. 'We're bloody lucky . . .'

A week on the road, in mid-summer heat, struggling—I suspected—from one oasis of refrigerated beer to the next, had taken high toll of Whiteley. His face had aged twenty years: an accumulation of morning-after faces, perhaps, each applied directly to the ruins of the previous morning-after beneath, with no time for repairs. His afro hair style needed re-perming; his Zapata moustache had lost definition, reclaimed, resumed, by the surrounding stubble. He looked his age, whatever it was.

I had no idea what was going on. Where was Reggie? And why would a middle-aged disc jockey want to play drums with a band of school kids? And travel two thousand miles wedged among amplifiers and beer cans to do it?

Also I was worried about Keller.

'We *might* be able to practise at night. After my lessons.'

My grandmother appeared framed in the rectangle of the front door, back-lit, drawn by the voices.

'Paul,' she called, squinting out into the half-darkness. 'Are you there? Is everything alright?'

'These are my friends, Gran. Members of my . . . ensemble.'

It seemed easiest to borrow my mother's term.

'This is Jimmy. Scott. And . . .'

'Richard,' Whiteley stepped towards the door, honey-voiced. 'From the radio station. I'm looking after the boys in town. I wondered, Mrs Wallace, if the ensemble might practise here. For a few days. Just until the concert.'

'We're very loud,' I warned.

'I remember once hearing the 1812 Overture in the old soundshell,' Gran began.

'Ta, muchly,' Whiteley interrupted, then turned: 'Bring the stuff in.'

'I don't understand,' I cornered Scott and Jimmy inside the house, with Whiteley out of earshot, fetching in another drum fragment. 'Is Reggie crook?'

'He *was* looking sick when we left,' Jimmy snorted, and laughed.

Scotty seemed more concerned: 'There wasn't room in the van, Paul. We took a vote. Reggie went along with it. We *need* Rick—he has contacts in the South.'

'Reggie could have *flown* down. What about the money from the air fares?'

'We spent the money already. New amps. A mixer. And the van needed some work.'

'Then *Whiteley* should have flown down. He's got money coming out his ears.'

'He's got nothing,' Jimmy said. 'He's been sacked. And you lay off him, Paul. He's a good mate.'

'*Me* lay off *him*?' I began—and finished, as Whiteley appeared in the door.

Much of that first evening was spent in makeshift cleaning and repairs. The various bits of drum meccano no longer wished to fit together. The new amplifier facings were warped and blistered; the speaker boxes were clogged with dust, the first guitar chord that Scotty struck exploded a fine, red cloud into the air, further smaller puffs following with each chord.

We laughed, loudly, together, suddenly more at ease.

'Which way did you come? Straight across the desert?'

'There were a few detours.'

I wrenched open a window: 'I suppose we could use it on the Big Night. Something to grab attention. Fill the speakers with dust.'

'Fill your own speakers with dust,' Jimmy growled.

'Think about it. A publicity gimmick. The band from the bush . . .'

But the artistic direction of the band had passed out of my hands somewhere between Darwin and Adelaide.

'You're not a bunch of hicks,' Whiteley said. 'You're a *rock band*. Professional musos. Where you come from doesn't matter.'

'Fine,' I said. 'Forget it. But I've some other ideas. Rock arrangements of some classical melodies. I wondered what you thought.'

'Let's hear them.'

I banged out a rough, syncopated version of the Chopin I'd been practising with Keller all week. The melodies had fixed themselves in my mind, an irritating background noise that I couldn't shake off, a stuck record playing the same phrases again and again. By distorting them, I hoped I might exorcise those sounds.

'Nice beat,' Whiteley commented.

'Ta, muchly,' I parodied him, bravely.

'But you're trying to do too much. Rock music is always simple.'

He paused, and added another familiar line from his repertoire of radio patter: 'A trap for young players.'

'Not our scene, Paul,' Scotty added, a little awkwardly.

'Did I show you my tattoo?' Jimmy was pulling off his jacket, trying to change the subject: an act of tact and sensitivity I would have put beyond him. 'Don't touch—it's still swollen.'

I chose not to demonstrate my Chopin improvements to Keller when he arrived the following morning. Nor did I make any reference to the set of drums parked between the two pianos, or the rest of the equipment scattered about the room. As always I was determined to keep my two musical worlds apart, certain they were immiscible.

He also said nothing—until, rising to leave, he collided gently with a cymbal and set it softly shimmering.

'Ah, yes,' he said. 'Drums.'

He nodded knowingly: 'If your neighbour offends you, give his children gifts of drums.'

'I beg your . . .?'

He stepped down hard on the bass drum pedal: PUM.

'Ancient Chinese proverb,' he said.

He paused again as he passed the electric keyboard pushed deep into a corner, half-hidden.

'Every fish has its depth,' he murmured, then headed off in search of his daily fix of newsprint, without looking back, leaving me puzzling over the phrase for hours.

———— ◆ ————

We waited backstage in the Glenelg Town Hall for our collective name to be called. The small side room was fogged out with cigarette smoke, and the smoke of other herbs, and crowded with musicians who all seemed nearer to Whiteley's age than to ours. Leather jackets and mirror sunglasses were of no help here. Taste had moved on to cooler, more casual styles: loose Eastern shirts, sandals, rimless glasses. The temperature of the music we could hear from the stage had cooled too . . .

I could feel their absurd hopes of fame and fortune drain from Scott and Jimmy as they sat huddled together in a self-protective leather kraal. Even Whiteley was silent for once, sitting slightly apart from us, distracted, clutching his drumsticks, perhaps wondering exactly how he had got so quickly out of touch.

I tried to distract Jimmy. 'When are you going back?'

'Might do a few gigs,' he said. His vocabulary resembled Whiteley's more and more each day. 'Rick has contacts. Then we'll head east. A slow trip up the coast. Rick heard about some radio job in Newcastle . . .'

'What about you?' Scotty asked. 'Thought about coming with us?'

'I wouldn't fit in the van.'

He laughed, guiltily: 'Tell Reggie I'm sorry.'

'I'll tell him,' I said. 'I fly home the day after the piano competition.'

'Think you've got a chance?'

'More than we've got here,' my tongue wanted to say, but at the last moment chose to follow orders.

'Maybe,' I said instead. 'You coming to listen?'

'Where is it?' Jimmy put in.

'The Conservatorium. In the City.'

I paused, watching them check each other's expressions. I let them off the hook. 'It's not compulsory,' I said.

'It's not our scene.' Scotty was spokesman. 'We'd just get in the way. But good luck.'

It was a parting of the ways, I sensed—a foreshadowing of the break-up of the band even before it had played. The knowledge was on us quickly, without warning, and we tried our best to prepare: saying our goodbyes, reassuring each other that, yes, we'd had some great times. And having done so we rose when our collective name was called and walked out onto the stage, and plugged in our various instruments and played together for the last time—or more apart than together: loudly, awkwardly, unenthusiastically.

Afterwards, side-stage, nothing remained to be said. The boys planned to drown their troubles in some bar that would fail to recognise their age. Whiteley knew a club they might try—some health club in the city, Men Only. And so I left them, bequeathing my electric keyboard to the remnants of the band, not bothering to wait for the announcement of results.

I needed an early night. Keller was arriving early the following morning, and the next two days held far more promise for me than this world of squalid, foolish dreams.

He noticed immediately the absence of the drums.

'The dance band is gone?'

It was the first direct mention he had made.

'It's not a *dance* band.'

'You play dance music, no?'

'We play rock'n roll.'

'Ah, yes—rock and roll. That is more a . . . fast march? Common time. With major sevenths. Like this . . .'

I'll never forget that image of him: the ancient brick-faced Viennese virtuoso in his white suit, belting out twelve bars of fast blues.

'Good music,' he nodded, approvingly. 'It simplifies. Prevents thought. Gives easy orders . . .'

I sat silently, waiting.

'You wish to play this music instead? In the Piano Competition?'

'It's over,' I said. 'We lost.'

'We never lose,' he chided me. 'We only learn.'

Here Endeth The Lesson, I mouthed silently. For the first time I found his neat packages of advice glib, predictable, even irritating. He smiled at me: a knowing, all-wise Confucian smile, and I felt an urge to blaspheme.

'We'll win it next year,' I said. 'When I get a decent electric piano. And a bigger amplifier.'

He worked me late that night, partly as punishment no doubt. For the first time he remained for dinner: eating with some difficulty the allegedly 'German' sausages that Gran had bought and kept frozen for this eventuality.

I was still working at my keyboard at midnight when I glanced across to find him fast asleep at the other piano, in sitting position, his red, grizzled head slumped forward on his chest . . .

Gran had the spare bed in my room encased in her best linen within minutes, and a pair of spare pyjamas neatly folded on the pillow. Against Keller's sleepy protestations, she manoeuvred him towards the room.

'I must summon a taxi, dear lady.'

'Nonsense. It's far too late, Mr Keller. We would be honoured if you would accept our hospitality.'

His presence seemed to produce a kind of stilted, archaic speech from her, as if it were contagious.

'A token of our esteem.'

He rose early the following morning. The sun was barely up, the traffic still silent, the only sound a single dove warbling softly, repetitively, somewhere. Watching him struggle free of the bedclothes, his joints seized up in the cold air, I realised for the first time how old he was.

Oh, I knew the figures, the birth year—knew that he was eighty-one, perhaps eighty-two. But somehow he'd always seemed younger: frozen in that indeterminate common age of alcoholics, the pickled late middle age they remain suspended in until death.

Watching him that morning I recognised him for the first time as the octogenarian he was, a whole generation older even than my grandparents.

After bathing and shaving he returned to the room, wrapped in towels, and began to pull on the various complicated jigsaw pieces of white linen and elastic that my grandmother had spent the small hours of the night ironing and starching. I spied on him secretly from bed: the thin, undernourished legs; the belly swollen by booze; the dark terracotta of the face suddenly becoming white flesh at the neckline as if he had been moulded from pale putty, or white clay, and only the topmost portion had been fired.

Then he lifted his arm to tug a garment into place, and for the first and only time I saw the number.

Tattooed on the pale hairless skin of his left forearm, just above the watchline: six faded blue digits.

And then just as suddenly the tattoo was gone, a shirt sleeve yanked over it, a cuff being firmly buttoned down.

'You were a prisoner in the War?' I blurted out.

'Everyone was a prisoner in the War,' he murmured, dismissively.

'I didn't know,' I said. 'Was your wife with you? Which camp?'

He continued dressing in silence.

'What was it called?'

'There were many camps,' he finally muttered, and rose and left the room. 'Their name is always the same.'

——— ◆ ———

*O*ur weekly consultations resumed on our return from the South. At first I suspected that Keller was disappointed in me, but his emotional climate might easily have been part of his annual mood cycle: a reflection of the arrival of November, and the worst dog-days of the Wet. A great weight of humidity pressed down once again on the town, a pressure that seemed to force him back into his shuttered room, brooding, flicking through his scrapbooks, drinking endlessly from his flask of schnapps.

It was only now that I realised he had not drunk at *all* in Adelaide.

'I could have played better,' I tried to persuade him.

He shook his head: 'No. We prepared fully.'

'I'll practise more next time.'

'No. Next time—less.'

His advice teased at me, as always. What could he mean? Which way to take it? I hoped all would become clear the night he accepted—for only the second time in two years—my parents' invitation to dinner, to discuss my future.

High school was finishing; the educational resources of Darwin could take me no further. Adrift in the timelessness of childhood, the dwindling weeks of that year still seemed a lifetime to me, but to my parents my predicament worsened each week. Thick Syllabus Guides from various Southern universities began appearing in the house, scattered casually about the front room, like coffee-table books, for light reading.

'Medicine in Adelaide looks interesting,' my father might suggest, thumbing through.

'Anything but medicine.' My mother had her own ideas. 'Law in Melbourne? Rosie will be in Melbourne. And you could take Music as an extra.'

'Languages perhaps. You enjoy languages, Paul.'

Suggestions were handed back and forth between them, new arguments and rationalisations produced, positions swapped. And through all the talk one thing rapidly emerged, unsaid: they no longer felt they had a concert pianist on their hands. A music teacher, perhaps . . . but not a performer. I had managed only a distant third place in Adelaide, and their disappointment was clear to me—even, or perhaps especially, when they pretended otherwise.

The two winners, they never tired of reminding me, and themselves, were so much *older*.

My mother did her best that night. Once again the food was Viennese, or as near to Viennese as the markets of Darwin allowed: schnitzel, potatoes, homemade sauerkraut—left over from the year before, she joked—and a bottle of some Hungarian-style wine that my father had got his hands on somewhere.

All of which, as before, was wasted on Keller. As my parents began discussing the merits of various music schools in the Southern states he cut them short:

'Enough of this stool polonaise.'

'Musical chairs,' I interpreted, familiar with the expression, one of his favourites.

'A conservatorium can teach him nothing,' he said.

'How do you mean, Herr Keller?'

'It will make him an adequate teacher—if he so wishes.'

I nurtured vague ideas of something more ambitious:

'What about Julliard? Or the London School of Music? What about Europe?'

'Europe has come to you,' Keller said. 'Europe has nothing more than this to offer.'

And he held out his two hands, palm up.

'Perhaps Paul has to discover that for himself,' my mother said, annoyed by the man's certainty.

He smiled: 'Perhaps. I wished only to save him time. A small hurt now to avoid a wasted life.'

'It's not fair,' I said. 'To make these decisions on the basis of one competition.'

'It is *not* the competition,' Keller told me. 'You should have won the competition. You were the best.'

This was the news to me, the first I'd heard of his judgement. My spirits rose.

'They *want* me to study at the Conservatorium,' I said.

'What else can they teach you?'

To play with feeling, I almost said. With abandon. To play Rachmaninoff and Liszt. To play Liszt's transcriptions of Wagner.

'What is the difference between a great and a good pianist?' I asked him, repeating one of his favourite questions.

'Not much,' he admitted. 'Little bits.'

'What if I stayed *here*. Learnt from you. Could you teach those little bits?'

'Perhaps,' he said. 'Perhaps not. We would need many years. It is always a gamble. You are my best student, yes. One in a thousand. But a concert pianist is one in a *million*.'

'I want to stay.'

'We will discuss it,' my father murmured, but I could already hear *his* decision, as I'm sure could Keller, who, if he was disappointed, managed to hide it with as much thoroughness as he hid everything he felt.

'More wine, Herr Keller?'

'Please.'

113

I should have taken a greater part in that discussion; made a more forceful stand. But in the end, none of it seemed important enough. I was not yet involved in my future imaginatively or emotionally; the future was still too far off. I dreamt of New York and Vienna, yes—but there seemed plenty of time. I was content to let others make decisions that in no way seemed important, or pressing, or irreversible—yet.

More pressing was the possibility of snatching a few minutes at Rosie's after dinner. Rain was falling outside; the perfumes of the earth folded back on themselves and multiplied. The rich, dank air filled my nostrils; I wanted to be out in the warm rain, pushing through the wet vegetation, physically part of it. That world and I were moulded from the same substances, I knew: we shared the same pollens, scents, sexual triggers, the same cycles of fertility; the same *molecules*. As my father talked wine I closed my eyes and listened to the sounds of the night, to the wet earth smearing itself with greenness: the thickly spread jam of tropical life, a vast croaking, rustling, crawling abundance.

And thus, while I listened, the future became the present, unchallenged; and all too soon the regretted past.

———◆———

I visited the dark shuttered room above the beer garden in the *Swan* for the last time the night before I left for the South. School was finally over; Life about to start. My entire class seemed to be flying off in the small, hot hours of that night: Rosie to Melbourne, to study medicine; Megan Murray to Art School in Sydney; Bennie Reid—a surprise for everyone—to Naval Officer Training School, Nowra.

A giant party of bonfires and forbidden booze was planned on Casuarina Beach: a last farewell to the carefree life we still only half sensed was passing from us. The distance that remained for us to travel together had shrunk to hours, but the end was still not squarely faced, not yet fully imagined.

And yet I somehow knew that all that Darwin had meant to me would be contracted and distilled into that last night: pinned in my memory like one of Bennie's flawlessly mounted butterflies.

I arranged for Rosie to collect me from the *Swan* at eight sharp—I did not want to be late.

Both piano lids in Keller's room were closed: the first time I had ever seen this. He was sitting in his armchair when I entered—facing a second armchair, a new chair which I had never seen before, and could only believe was bought new for the occasion.

'Sit,' he gestured gruffly.

A small coffee table had apparently also been purchased; two empty glasses waited on the polished surface. As I sat, my teacher filled each glass with several fat fingers, or thumbs, of neat schnapps.

'Our hours together are over,' he said, and drank.

My throat clogged with a painful lumpiness which I tried to blame on the schnapps. Or perhaps that lump was words: suddenly I found I had nothing to say, could produce no recognisable noise.

'You have enrolled?' he finally asked. 'In Adelaide?'

I nodded, reluctantly: 'Law. And music—performance. I *wanted* to stay here.'

'It is good that you are not staying,' he finally said. 'I also wanted you to stay: but for me, not for you.'

I sat with my eyes fixed on the polished woodgrain of the coffee table.

'*You* are my teacher,' I said. 'You've been like a father to me. Taught me everything I know.'

He raised a quibbling finger: 'I have taught you everything you were able to learn.'

I couldn't believe my ears: our last hour together and he wanted to insult me. The rush of feeling I had felt for him, the warm lump in the throat, vanished.

'I don't mean to hurt you,' he said. 'But better a small hurt now . . .'

'Than a wasted life,' I finished for him, tersely. 'Yes, I know.'

'You are very talented,' he said. 'But.'

I waited, but he said no more.

'But?'

'A small word containing many small things.'

He refilled his schnapps glass for the third time.

'However,' he murmured at length, 'my affection for you does not depend on those small things.'

Affection? To hear him admit it, to actually utter words of love, however understated, astonished me.

'I once had great plans for my own son, Eric,' he said. 'I had begun to teach him—he showed great promise. Perhaps I have been too hard on you because of that. A father's hardness.'

'You never speak of him. Or of your wife.'

'It is . . . unspeakable.'

I glanced at my watch: 7.55. I wanted to know more, but at what price? Rosie might already be waiting, parked in the street. I knew she would be wearing nothing underneath— her face had blushed with excited shame as she had told me the day before . . .

'They died in the War?'

'They died *during* a War. The War was incidental.'

He poured out another drink, downing the clear fluid in a rapid, almost continuous series of sips. I gained the impression he was fortifying himself, gathering strength.

'You know a little perhaps of the history of my country? You have heard of Dollfuss? Of the Anschluss?'

'No.'

'You have heard perhaps of Hitler?'

'Of course,' I bristled.

'Herr Hitler was an artist. Like you. Like me.'

This seemed to border on the incoherent. How much schnapps had he downed before my arrival?

'No-one in Vienna enjoyed his art. He left a bitter man. Later he came back—with many friends.'

I didn't know whether this childish schoolyard version— history reduced to schoolyard politics—was for my benefit, or served some ironic, drunken purpose of his own.

'I know a little . . .' I began.

He laughed, quickly, harshly: 'You *cannot* know. But that is no matter.'

Here was the first sign of passion in his measured words.

'Nothing changed at first,' he continued. 'Not in my world. But later, yes. People began disappearing. My friends began disappearing. But slowly. Many had left of course. Jewish friends.'

'I know that,' I said, my back up, still wounded by his earlier remarks. 'I've read books. I'd rather know why *you* stayed. I asked you once—you refused to answer.'

He looked up, the jelly of his eyes moist and red: 'I was not Jewish.'

'Your wife was Jewish.'

He shrugged, but I knew that I had touched—with the insensitivity of the hurt—the heart of the matter:

'Who would harm the wife of Eduard Keller?' he said.

Half of me wanted to remain, to quiz him further, to fit these various bits and pieces of wartime biography together; but half of me wanted to be out of there, now. I felt 'affection' for him certainly—I *loved* him, in many ways—but I loved Rosie more.

'Did *she* wish to leave?' I pressed, and heard a slow exhalation from him, a sigh of relaxation, or release. I had the feeling that he had *wanted* me to ask him this question, to interrogate him further.

'There was no future for her. No engagements. No invitations. Snubbed by former friends, music directors . . .'

'So you *did* finally leave?'

'The evil would pass, I told her. All things pass.'

He was gazing at the portrait on the piano, but I was listening to a car tooting in the street: a sound of enormous sexual gravity.

Only now can I recognise the scene for what it was: a confessional, a privilege that I, through selfishness and sensual addiction, failed to accept. Nothing had yet been explained. What had happened to his wife? And their son? And what of *his*—Keller's—tattooed serial number? And why, after all these years, had he decided to entrust *me* with this immense secret, this weight he wanted to heave from his soul?

'Besides,' he continued. 'Things improved. Briefly. In . . . 1938.'

I should have stayed, listened, poured out his schnapps, lubricated his tongue. But there wasn't enough time. The aroused, sexual present overwhelmed the past.

'Eichmann arrived back in Vienna. You have also perhaps heard of Eichmann?'

'Of course,' I repeated. 'The murderer.'

'A most charming man.' Keller wasn't listening to me. 'And *most* efficient. The head of the Centre for Emigration of Austrian Jews. He released many prominent people from prison. He organised concerts: fundraising for the emigrés.'

'So you could have left?'

'I was assured,' he stumbled on. 'Jewish members of German families would not be harmed. And the child—our mongrel, our *mischling*—he was safe. Privileged . . .'

I was on my feet.

'I have to be off,' I lied. 'My plane. But I'll write soon. Let you know how I'm going.'

He rose unsteadily, and clutched my proffered hand between both his small, manicured paws.

'You must understand,' he said. 'I *knew* these people. These murderers. I had signed their concert programmes.'

I moved a step back, tugging slightly, but he failed to release me, and our clasped hands swung up awkwardly between us, a straining hawser.

'There were rumours, of course,' he stumbled on. 'Death squads in Poland. But I couldn't believe them.'

'I'll never forget you,' I blustered. 'You'll be the first I invite to hear me play at the Sydney Opera House. I'll fly you down.'

'You will understand,' he said. 'Perhaps not now, but soon. Vienna was my home. It is more difficult to see evil in your own home. So much is familiar, reassuring—what can happen? The Nazis arrived, and what was different? Ninety nine per cent of our lives remained the same.'

'It was the other one per cent that mattered,' I said, knowing that if I hadn't, he would have.

The car tooted again, more insistently, in the street outside. I shook myself suddenly free and walked down the wooden steps, a little dizzy with schnapps, filing away the horrific fragments of story he had told me for later, trying to focus at the time only on Rosie, and the party.

I turned at the base and I looked back at him, standing at the top of the stairs above the beer garden. A grim smile had returned to his face.

'I do not tell you this for me,' he called down, shouting above the noise of the drinkers. 'But for you.'

He raised his right hand, more a gesture of dismissal than a farewell wave. His gold ring caught the light, glinting.

'You never told me,' I called back up. 'What happened to your finger?'

'It offended me,' he said.

He paused, examining his hand as if it were some odd, distasteful object, turning it this way and that.

'But I could not—how do you say?—finish the job,' he added, and turned away, back towards his room and his schnapps.

1974

The years that followed in Adelaide, at the Conservatorium, passed so slowly, so monotonously, that the retelling of them can only pass quickly. My Law studies soon fell by the wayside—early successes encouraged me to concentrate on Music instead. I left a trail of prizes behind me . . . and also a trail of teachers. Keller had spoiled me, I soon began to realise. I quickly tired of the second-rate, and the first-rate tired equally quickly of me and my rigid second-hand opinions.

Everything he had taught me—every opinion, every phrasing, every note—had hardened into dogma. Things I had thought laughable when he first uttered them now seemed profound, part of a musical Bible whose texts I knew by heart and quoted freely, especially when speaking through my hands. The gospel of Czerny and Liszt had been handed on to me personally; I hectored my fellow students and teachers with its texts cruelly.

'How do *you* know Liszt meant the piece to be played like that?'

'Liszt told Leschetizky. Who told Keller. Who told me.'

I was smug, insufferable—and far better at playing the piano than anyone else.

My parents moved South in my second year of study, finally tiring of life in the tropics: the Wet season too hot for my mother; the Dry too parched for my father's small grove of withered rambutan and mangosteen seedlings.

Perhaps also—I liked to think—they missed their son, or wanted to bask in his performances, share in the eisteddfod prizes, the exam results.

My father left the Government Medical Service, buying a cheap general practice in the leafy suburbs. His hobby farm, he called it: a once-busy practice whose patients had grown old and were rapidly dying off, preceded by their former doctor. My mother found part-time library work to supplement their dwindling income.

Both of them, as always, were far more interested in music. Together they joined, and soon commandeered, the local suburban Gilbert and Sullivan Society.

'*The Mikado* this year?'
'I think *The Gondoliers.*'
'I must insist . . .'
'Please. It's *my* turn to choose.'
'Let me choose the opera, and you can choose your part . . .'

I remember those years, like all the years of my childhood, as a kind of Gilbert and Sullivan version of the Chinese calendar: the Year of the Mikado, the Year of the Pirate, the Year of the Gondolier, the Year of the Pinafore—and the cycle would start all over again.

And Keller? Although I quoted him tirelessly through those years in Adelaide I wrote to him infrequently. I knew enough, I'd decided. I'd learnt all the lessons that were in his power to teach me. On the few occasions I did write, his answer always came promptly; but now his advice seemed irrelevant, long behind me, useful only for those snippets I could repeat, loudly, in lessons and Master Classes.

No advance in art is possible for the self-satisfied . . . A step back is often as useful as a step forward . . .

At the end of 1972—a Year of the Gondolier—I sent him a tape of my Honours performance in Elder Hall, a Christmas gift which I expected him to treasure: Bach, Mozart, Debussy—and Grandfather Liszt. I was stunned to receive the tape back in the post the following week, together with a thick wodge—no, a *book*—of notes, a critique that tore my performance apart phrase by phrase.

That first morning I could read only the first page before tossing it aside, overcome by anger . . .

'Did he like the cassette, dear?' My mother poked her head through my bedroom door.

'Very much,' I lied.

'It was a thick parcel. Did he send you a Christmas gift?'

'Um . . . yes,' I improvised. 'Some sheet music.'

'Could I see the letter? I always like to read his letters. So does your father.'

I wanted to turn and scream at her, to loosen my hatred on the nearest meddling scapegoat.

'If I can find it,' I managed to limit myself. 'I know I left it around here somewhere.'

Back to basics for Bach. I sank deeper into the letter that night. *Six months of The Children's Bach, Small Preludes, Inventions. Then, perhaps, the 48. But you must learn all over again the separation of the voices. Separate and together . . .*

The *Children's* Bach? Still? I was now a well-known pianist in a medium-large city—playing the Tchaikovsky Concerto with the Youth Orchestra the following week—and some small-town drunk has-been wanted me to play kindergarten pieces. I lay in bed reading restlessly, twitching and thrashing about, winding myself in my bedsheets in my fury. *Do not play Debussy again for several months. Listen to Gieseking, then start over again. I do not mean you to play like Gieseking, but from him you have much to learn . . .*

I crumpled the letter into a tight ball, and tossed it into the bin. Let Gieseking listen to *me*—if he was still alive. *I* was the only pianist I had time to listen to.

I retrieved the crumpled letter from the bin the following morning, unpeeled the ball of paper carefully, like a mandarin, then read through to the end, as if it were some thriller, repulsive, but unable to be left alone.

It would be so much easier to play for you than to explain. A few seconds on the piano speaks so much more than pages of writing . . .

An invitation, certainly—but one I chose not to find between the lines at the time. Christmas was closing fast; two months of vacation lay ahead. I could—I *should*—have travelled North, but I travelled east instead, to Rosie and Melbourne. All my holidays were spent in her shared students' house there: making love, concert-going, socialising with her small circle of medical student friends, practising on the cheap Korean piano wedged into a corner of her bedroom while she worked at her various part-time waitressing jobs.

I loved her—which, at a time when most of my love was wasted on myself, was no small achievement. Those nights of deepest, first-discovered joy in Darwin had never left us; each term's separation only magnified our memory, and desire.

And so the choice that Christmas was simple: two months with *The Children's Bach* in Darwin, or two months with Rosie in Melbourne.

I chose Rosie: her bedroom full of thick textbooks and fragments of human bones and candle-lit love was my favourite hiding-hole, and her house—full of friends, part-time musicians mostly, quiet intellectual types who gathered in the bedroom each night to hear me play, listening with serious rapture, and believing me the new Horowitz, or Rubinstein—was my favourite home.

——— ◆ ———

I was overseas through Christmas, 1974, performing. Or so I liked to tell people. Overseas, performing: the two words still slide easily from my tongue, affecting a glamour far greater than I deserved.

I was not so much performing as competing: leap-frogging across the planet from Piano Competition to Piano Competition, part of a travelling circus of would-be concert artists who chased fame and prize money from San Francisco to New York to Warsaw to Munich to Tokyo, hoping for the Main Chance . . .

A Two Year Plan. I had bargained for it with my parents— who finally agreed, impressed by my performances and exam results. They even put up the larger share of the money, mortgaging their new home. One year to learn the ropes, I argued: one year to become a familiar face, a fixture, and a second year to see how far I could go. It was a gamble, of course—a musical lottery, Keller had often called it—but a lottery whose odds could be shortened, and whose First Prizes meant Instant Career. I realised even then that I would have regretted all my life not taking that gamble. As also— despite their doubts—would my parents. They had wanted a concert pianist in the family for years. The Dream would have itched away at them, lingering, nagging, still possible. Could he have? What if?

Full of myself at first, my enthusiasm slowly faded. The months lengthened, the excuses multiplied: injured hands, insufficient practice time, junk pianos, unqualified juries. And the name Eduard Keller opened no doors to me: after the disaster of my first competition in Paris, I quickly dropped any mention of Keller from my *curriculum vitae.*

The juries had either not heard of him, or thought me some sort of confidence man or impostor.

'You learnt piano through a medium, perhaps, Monsieur Crabbe? In a seance? You can communicate with the dead?'

To explain myself proved impossible: it seemed I could translate anything into French except the truth, at least in the brief time I was allowed to offer an explanation.

'A misprint,' I quickly surrendered. 'I belonged to Keller's *school*, in the broad sense. My *teacher* learnt from Keller.'

Lost in my private world of ambition and keyboards and excuses, my tunnel vision limited to the next hotel booking, the next deadline for audition tapes, the next connecting flight, that year I lost all contact with newspapers. A letter from my father tracked me down *poste restante* in Salzburg in the early New Year, bringing news of the cyclone, Tracy, and the terrible total destruction of the town of Darwin on Christmas Eve.

Keller had survived the storm, my father wrote, and was now their house guest in Adelaide, temporarily: an evacuee awaiting return to Darwin. If and when . . .

He sent his warm regards, my father relayed. Also a little familiar-sounding advice, penned at the end of the letter: *Don't put too much store on winning—you never win by much.*

I found this irritating—and also contradictory. I remembered well his earlier question: what is the difference between good and great? His repertoire of advice resembled the Bible especially in this: one text could always be quoted to annul another if it proved inconvenient.

The letter reached me at lowest ebb—trying to convalesce after yet another Honourable Mention in a minor competition. Honourable Mention had become the story of my life, no matter how much I practised. I had found my level, my performances frozen into a recurring pattern of Also Rans.

You don't win by much? I scribbled angrily on a sheet of hotel notepaper. *You win by three years of solid bookings and engagements. You win by a fat contract with Deustsche Grammophon, or EMI. You win by . . .*

I didn't send this note. Rosie's weekly letter from Melbourne arrived the following day: and those letters always possessed powers of healing. I liked to think of them as a kind of prescription, written as part of her medical training. She followed my travels keenly, collecting the results and programme notes and clippings that I mailed to her in a thick scrapbook—her 'Form Guide'—and sending by return mail her hopes and prayers and promises. She always seemed able to tell me exactly what I wanted to hear.

The other competitors were so much older and more experienced . . . Of course the Russian won. Two of the judges were Russian . . .

More details of the cyclone followed from my father in his next letter. Our old house had gone, someone who knew someone who had a friend who was there had told him: blown down into the gully and across the tidal mudflats out to sea. Rumours were rife of mass beach graves containing far more than the official death toll. But the letter finished with an image I would never forget, an image of such strangeness and poetry that I spent weeks thinking about it, picturing it, searching it for significance.

Eduard Keller had survived the worst of the storm, my father wrote, by sheltering beneath the supine, beneath his grand piano, his beloved *Bösendorfer*, wet and shivering and lacerated by flying glass as the roof lifted off the *Swan*, and the walls of his room disintegrated about him, but safe beneath that grand piano . . .

I could imagine him snorting with amusement as he was pulled clear: 'So the piano *is* finally useful for something . . .'

Vienna, 1975

I was beached in Europe at the time, stranded between one competition and the next. On Rosie's advice I had visited Salzburg; trekked through the winter snows from various Birthplaces to Performances to Gravestones, more out of obligation to her and to my parents—who were still footing the bill, and who used me as a surrogate tourist—than for myself. I heard Brendel at the Mozarteum, Badura-Skoda in the New Festspielhaus, listening to both through the usual fog of envy and technical quibbling that made any enjoyment of their music impossible.

From there I railroaded myself to Krems, on the Danube: taking a short-term piano tutoring position at some kind of holiday finishing school, after answering an advertisement stuck on a noticeboard in the Mozarteum. The first year of travelling had taught me where to look for such things; there was always a little extra pocket-money to be found between competitions. The work was lonely: a succession of bored, untalented students entered and left my small room all day on the half-hour; and three times each day meals were taken in a cold dining room at a Head Table, lost among the sounds of a foreign language and a staff who had all known each other for years.

At nights my thoughts in this crowded monastery kept returning to Keller. That vision of him sheltering from the hurricane beneath his grand piano returned to me, pricked at me—and always at the back of my mind was the knowledge that Vienna was no more than an hour's distance. I had asked the occasional question about him during my travels, had visited the odd library—but my mind was always elsewhere. Now for the first time my self-preoccupations had diminished enough. I decided to try to begin piecing together the various fragments of his life, beginning with what he'd told me during our last conversation together.

Sitting in my cold room in Krems I began writing letters to Vienna in a pidgin German which I laundered through the more obliging of my pupils: letters to vague musical acquaintances, to former competitors, to the musical journals, and finally to institutions: the Staatsakademie, the Conservatoire, the Nationalbibliothek, and the Library at the Old Universität, asking only that my letters be pinned to the bulletin boards for a few days.

Loneliness, linguistic seclusion, and the four grim walls of my bedroom study seemed to find some paranoid core in me, and feed it. For reasons I still don't fully understand I adopted a mask in those letters, resorted to vague subterfuge—feigning an interest in the piano school of Leschetizky, with a particular interest in writing a brief biography of his student Eduard Keller, and asking for any anecdotes, reminiscences, letters that might prove valuable. I had seen such letters from earnest erstwhile biographers in journals many times.

Various notes trickled back in the following weeks, but only two contained mentions of Keller. The first told me nothing I hadn't known, quoting back at me the false footnote I had found years before in Adelaide—that Keller had died in 1944.

The other was far more thrilling: a note in an unsteady hand, but in flawless, stylised English, from a cellist, Joseph Henisch, who claimed to have played Trios with Keller before the War. He was most gratified—he wrote—that a biography was planned: Keller was the pianist and teacher he himself had 'prized above all others of his generation'; and 'an artist who had suffered more than any man had a right to suffer'.

I read this last passage twice, packed and shouldered my bags and music, and walked out of my room and my job, down half a mile of cobbled streets to the Danube, and floated on the next ferry downstream to Vienna.

—— ◆ ——

I had never carried a camera, despite my parents' and Rosie's urgings, arguing—self-importantly—that I wanted nothing to come between me and the 'pure' experience.

My precious, priceless experiences.

When pressed, I mailed picture postcards to Australia:

standard views of Towers Eiffel or Leaning, Islands Emerald or Aegean, accompanied always by the excuse that these were of far higher quality than anything *I* could hope to produce.

But Vienna brought out the tourist skulking deep within, set me gaping, muttering inanities to myself, reaching for a non-existent camera . . .

I had never set foot in the city before, but every street corner brought small shocks of rediscovery, realisations of things I hadn't known I *knew*: the familiar features of that dream city of music and dusty history which I had put together in my head, from books, in the Library of the University of Adelaide many years before. I wandered through the Staatsoper, the Rathaus, the maze of the Wiener Hofburg, needing no tour-guide but myself.

I recalled Herr Keller's words of contempt when trying to dampen my enthusiasm.

'Old Vienna vanished long ago,' he often told me, a quote I suspected he had borrowed from somewhere. 'It was demolished into a Great City.'

And again: 'A city designed for military pomp and cavalcades.'

I believed him even less now than then.

Henisch, the cellist, lived in a small third-floor apartment in Neubau, on Mariahilfer Strasse. (I write these placenames casually, as if I have lived among them all my life—and in many senses I *have* lived among them all my life.) We sat in his front room, amid wood panelling and furniture so dark and rich it might have been fashioned from disused cellos. A dark, upright piano in the corner also seemed fashioned from recycled cello-wood. The heavy drapes were drawn; the only light a dull golden-yellow filtered through two lampshades. The apartment smelt as the homes of elderly bachelors smell the world over: a mixture of dust and liniment and yesterday's cooking odours and—somewhere, always— a bowl of dried *potpourri*.

'It is strange,' Henisch was saying, 'that we need someone from so far away to teach us about our musicians.'

He was a small man, wearing rimless glasses, his face

leather-brown: not so much a smoker's face as a smoked face, each dark wrinkle carefully pickled, preserved. But no nicotine stained his fingers, nor was the smell of tobacco among those other familiar smells.

'Australia exports rice to Asia.' I small talked, remembering an article I had read somewhere at home, years before. 'We even export spaghetti to Italy.'

He smiled: 'And now musicologists to Vienna.'

A small, delicate pot of tea steamed on a side-table between us. Henisch leant forward, and filled two fragile blue cups.

'Lemon?'

'Please.'

'I am between lessons,' he continued. 'I would be happy to help in any way until then.'

'It was very good of you to see me,' I said, still not sure how to begin. 'You must be very busy.'

'Did you receive many answers,' he asked. 'To your requests?'

'Not many. But I could think of no other method.'

He smiled again: 'There are many who would like to forget.'

'But not you?'

'Eduard accompanied me many times,' he said. 'Of course he was the far greater musician . . . *far* greater. A virtuoso. There was no comparison between us. But that was a measure of his generosity.'

I untangled a notepad from my coat pocket, a small stage prop.

'Do you mind if I take notes?'

'Of course you must take notes.'

I found a pen deep in another pocket:

'Why would people want to forget?'

A knock came at the door before he could answer, and a small boy entered half-carrying, half-dragging a large cello case.

'Sit,' Henisch murmured. 'You are early and must wait today.'

'You knew his wife?' I asked as he turned back to me.

'She was much younger. My age.' He paused and smiled, as if amused by his own small show of vanity. 'Eduard was in his forties when they met. Between the Wars.'

He reached again for his dainty cup, and sipped.

'They were wonderful days. The Empire was gone, broken. We sat in the cafés planning the new world. Eduard was in great demand—the marriage had found something new in him, some . . . fountain.'

He closed his eyes, his cup still pressed to his lips. His glasses fogged over with steam.

I guessed that his eyes had remained closed beneath, not noticing. Then he gave a small start, set down the cup, removed the glasses and began polishing.

'Too soon things became difficult. The old hypocrisies. Sweetness and light. And then the horror.'

'The Nazis?'

'Of course. Orchestras shrank. Many emigrated, many were serving in the Army, many . . . disappeared. Europe was killing its musicians.'

'You remained?'

He shrugged. 'No money. The Nazis had to be paid. But worse: no country would take us without money, *Vorzeigegeld.*'

'Bribes at both ends?'

'And suddenly it was too late to leave,' he continued. 'There were safe places—for a time. A city within a city. False rooms. Cellars. Locked doors.'

'Herr Keller hid his wife?'

He laughed, a soft harshness: 'If only he had. But Eduard would have none of it. He had played for Hitler . . . so who would harm his wife and child?'

The information came suddenly, a disconcerting switch from the general to the particular.

'He played for *Hitler*? How could he do that?'

'How could he *not* do that?'

Henisch paused, allowing me time to think, to relocate my imagination from the gentle suburbs of Australia.

'A private performance was arranged,' he continued. 'Adolf Eichmann was in Vienna at the time. 1938 . . . You have perhaps heard of Eichmann?'

I remembered the same question from Keller, years before. 'A little.'

'He was very involved in musical circles—when he wasn't killing people. Eduard was flown to Berlin several times in his personal plane. Perhaps Eduard thought it would help save Mathilde.'

'She was a singer, wasn't she?'

'A Wagner specialist. And now the heirs of Wagner came and dragged her away.'

I had known, but was still horrified: 'Herr Keller let them take her?'

'He was in Berlin at the time. His last performance for Hitler . . . He blamed himself entirely.'

He sipped again at his tea. I reached for my cup also, not knowing what else to say.

'Do *you* blame him?' I eventually broke the silence.

Henisch shrugged: 'It is easy to blame now. He had two choices: to become invisible, or to become *so* visible that nothing could touch him.'

'And the son, Eric?'

He glanced to a corner of the room where his young student was fiddling with his cello, tightening strings, preoccupied. He lowered his voice:

'He refused to be parted from his mother.'

'They both died?'

'Died?' He laughed again, the same soft harshness. 'I do not like the word. It is too . . . acquiescent. They did not die. They were murdered.'

'And Herr Keller?'

'You are not taking notes,' he noticed.

I was frozen, hanging on every word. 'I do not need pen and paper. Tell me of Keller.'

His eyes met mine, and remained locked there, as if he wanted no misunderstanding: '*He* died.'

'I'm sorry?'

'He sewed the yellow star to his clothing on his return to Vienna. He registered as a Jew.'

I seemed to be learning too much too quickly. As he spoke

each astonishing sentence I was still grappling with some previous astonishing sentence.

'But Keller was not Jewish,' I tried to keep up.

'He no longer wished to be Austrian. He was transported in 1942.'

'I don't understand. He *pretended* to be Jewish? He *wanted* to be transported?'

Henisch sipped silently at his lemon-scented tea in its frail, exquisite cup.

'Some form of penance?' I guessed, trying to wrap my mind around it. 'Self-punishment?'

Henisch shrugged: 'Perhaps he felt he might find Mathilde and Eric—but he must have known. We *all* must have known. Rumours were everywhere that year.'

He paused, silent for a time: two minutes silence perhaps.

'Somehow he avoided the gas chambers. He was over fifty—but strong. Pianist's hands, shoulders. In early 1945 the Russians were closing on the camps. Transfers of the survivors began; removal of the evidence. Long marches: Auschwitz to Buchenwald. Buchenwald to Bergen–Belsen. Keller died on the last journey.'

For the moment I bit my tongue. If Keller wished to remain dead even to his friends, who was I to expose him?

'How do *you* know all this? That he died? How can you be sure?'

Henisch removed a stud from his shirt sleeve and jerked back the sleeve; on the outside of the leather-brown forearm I could see a tattoo, six digits, of which I remember only the first, a faded B.

I rose, my mind filled with a strange warfare of emotions, and paced restlessly.

I finally blurted it out. I *had* to blurt it out. 'What if I told you he survived? That he was my teacher in Australia?'

'Impossible, my young friend.'

'You saw his body?'

'A friend saw him fall. No-one who fell by the side lived.'

'But if I told you I *knew* him? That he lived in a hotel, in a town called Darwin? In the tropics. Teaching piano. You must have read about it—the hurricane. He's staying with my parents now, in the South. Have you a phone? I could *ring* him . . .'

A shrug answered me, then a smile: 'Keller is a common name.'

'How can I convince you? He always wears white. He has a finger missing from the right hand.'

He glanced up at me curiously, and I pressed on:

'I'm right, aren't I? He had no little finger?'

'Eduard had ten fingers. Of course. He was a pianist.'

He paused, his eyes becoming glazed, unfocused; or tuning perhaps to some different, internal focal length.

'But I remember,' he murmured. 'In the camps. There was a piano in the SS mess. A guard once asked him to play. Of course he refused—even if they had killed him he wouldn't play. But afterwards he told me . . . Do you wish to write this down?'

'No. Please. Go on.'

'He told me that if he ever felt the desire to play again he would hack off his fingers, one by one.'

'Then it *is* him.'

Henisch continued staring dreamily into space, more interested in the memories of the past I had awakened than in the possibility I was right. I paced back and forth, trying to find some final irrefutable proof of identification.

'He loves Bach and Mozart. And the later Beethoven. He hates the Romantics. Empty rhetoric, he calls it . . .'

At this Henisch returned suddenly to the present, shaking his head, smiling patiently, tolerantly: 'Eduard Keller would never play Mozart if he could play Liszt, or Rachmaninoff. He liked to entertain. He liked a big, strong sound.'

I found myself standing over the piano. I jerked up the lid and seated myself.

'No,' I said. 'I can prove it. Listen . . .'

Perhaps this was my finest performance ever, for an audience of one: Beethoven, the *Arietta* from Opus 111, a favourite of Keller's, a piece of immense complexity out of which, by some miracle, a state of immense simplicity is reached. I could have played far flashier, more athletic pieces—I could have played Liszt, or broken yet again the Minute Waltz—but I chose intellectual difficulty, instead. And *spiritual* difficulty. I wanted Henisch to understand that *I* understood. That I knew things that only Keller could have taught me.

He listened attentively at first, and perhaps I almost had him believing. But then I felt his attention wander. He refilled his teacup, and even—towards the end—leafed through a nearby magazine.

'Very fine,' he murmured as I slipped my hands from the keyboard, the sound of the last chords lingering there like a pair of forgotten gloves. 'Technically flawless. You obviously had a very fine teacher. But I am sorry: you did not learn from Eduard Keller. His students played with . . . with far more . . .'

Searching for words, he rose and pulled a record jacket from a shelf instead.

'More *rubato*,' he finally came out with, and handed me the record. 'Here—take this. I must begin my lessons. You are too young to have heard Eduard play. This was his last recording. In Munich, 1934.'

I was hurt, enormously—but that could be postponed till later. At the time I felt only anger. Henisch was a mere fiddler, I told myself—a scraper of catgut. What could he know of the piano?

'I couldn't possibly accept,' I said. 'You think I am lying . . .'

He smiled, sympathetically: 'I think you are mistaken. Take, I insist. I have others.'

I felt the weight of the disc in my hand; a thick, heavy 78. *Rapsodie Ungarische No. 3* was printed on one side, and on the other: *Wagner, Tristan und Isolde, Liebestod, transcr. Franz Liszt.*

I remembered clearly, instantly, Keller's words of contempt as he had tormentedly played that very same piece of music, years before: 'Music that film stars kiss to.' I couldn't believe my eyes. Or my ears:

'Eduard *loved* the Romantics,' Henisch was saying, but the words meant nothing to me. 'He was a passionate virtuoso.

Strength, and sonority. He made the instrument *sing*. Like his teacher before him.'

If we were discussing the same man, how different our two versions.

Or perhaps I *was* mistaken. Perhaps they were not the same man, in a sense.

1977

◆

*I*n late 1977 I received a letter from the charge sister of the hospice ward of Darwin Hospital, seeking information about the next of kin of Eduard Keller. Through her fog of clumsy assurances and euphemisms—he was In No Pain; he was Suffering a Long Illness—the truth quickly became clear . . .

I had corresponded frequently with him since my return from overseas. Teaching duties in Melbourne, marriage to Rosie and then the birth of our first child had prevented me making any trip North. I had made no mention in my letters of Vienna or of the meeting with Henisch—I felt, in part, that I had betrayed some sort of confidence by attempting to tell the world that he was still alive. If ever I confessed, it would have to be face to face.

As always, he was equally reticent in return: musical anecdotes, epigrammatic advice, news of the rebuilding of Darwin—these were the stuff of his short letters. There had been no mention of illness . . .

I flew North the following week, and perhaps that letter from the hospital was only a pretext, or catalyst. I had been wanting to return for some time, finding myself in times of depression and frustration dreaming more and more of those years in Darwin, or an idealised version of those years.

But first things first. I caught a taxi direct to the hospital from the airport, leaving my overnight bag dumped in the main entrance foyer.

Eduard Keller was sharing a room with two others in the same predicament: three dying men propped amid massed pillows, wasted even beyond the familiar standards of televised Starvation, staring at each other with a kind of glazed, drugged horror.

Was there meant to be some sort of comfort in Going Down Together: like ancient kings taking their households with them into the afterlife? To me it seemed more like a squalid Death Row: Death Row with flowers, and drugs.

And muzak. Unspeakable sounds oozed from a hidden loudspeaker somewhere, and a huge pressure of revulsion built in me as I listened:

Somewhe-e-re, over the rainbow . . .

'Sister,' I turned. 'Could we turn that off. *Please.*'

'Our clients find it very soothing, Mr Crabbe.'

At this Keller turned his head: 'Paul?'

His face had changed, lost character and uniqueness, become to some extent the common face of the dying. The incandescent redness had gone, the broken vessels seemed bleached, all colour had drained from the coarse, pitted skin. The eyes had sunken deeply, as if burrowing in.

'Wie gehts, Maestro,' I whispered, the word for the first time sounding upper-case in my mouth, respectful.

He smiled with difficulty: 'You have been practising.'

'My German a little rusty,' I managed, still in German.

'A Bavarian accent?'

'Too much time in München. Too little in Wien.'

I gripped his pale claw—a handful of frail bird-bones, so light it might have been fashioned from papier-mâché—and turned again to the sister:

'The muzak, Sister. For pity's sake . . .'

'It is nothing,' Keller murmured. 'Leave the music.'

'I could bring something else,' I suggested. 'Cassettes.'

An absurd list half-formed in my mind: Music to Die By. I remembered that precious 78 from Vienna, at home, wrapped in cottonwool. But no—he probably would have denied all knowledge of *that*. Mozart would be better: the *Requiem*, perhaps. The *Lacrimosa*. Or was that too obvious?

'Mozart?' I suggested. 'Something choral?'

His eyes had closed—beyond music, it seemed. Once he had valued Mozart above all others: Mozart shines like the sun, he would murmur, his face tilting upwards, slightly, as if towards some imagined source of light and warmth, his eyes shining.

I leant closer to his translucent, bluish ear:

'I remember you often used to say: silence is the purest music.'

There was no flicker of comprehension. His breathing had slowed: short sequences of shallow breaths interspersed by lengthy silences.

'He comes and goes,' the Sister whispered. 'The medication. He's usually at his best early in the morning.'

I sat by his bed listening to his faulty breathing till it seemed pointless to listen any longer, then collected my bag, and headed for the nearest hotel.

In the morning, at the hospice, nothing had changed; nor the morning after that. He died for another week in that public ward, in his private room of pain. I visited him before breakfast each day—usually with a book, or newspapers, to fill in the time. My role was unclear. He was aware of my presence from time to time; he might even accept the odd spoonful of soft, mashed food. I wanted to ask him many things, wanted even to tell him of Henisch, of what I had heard in Vienna . . . but any conversation beyond a description of his immediate needs was impossible. More often I read to him, even when he appeared to be sleeping: items from the papers of the type that had always interested him; poems from a book of German poetry I had found in a second-hand bookshop . . .

Where, when tired of wandering,
my last resting place will I find?
Under palm trees in the South?
Under lime trees on the Rhine?

Will I be buried somewhere
in a desert, by strange hands?
Or shall I rest beside
an ocean coast, in the sands?

No matter! Here, there, wherever,
God's heaven will surround me,
and all the stars of night
like funeral lamps hang over me.

Perhaps he would have sneered at such poetry, given full consciousness—suspicious, as always, of beauty, of the rhetoric of beauty. I wondered what had happened to his precious scrapbooks, and the thousands of stories of human foolishness and greed and cruelty that he had tried to patch together into some kind of understanding of his fellow beings. That, too, was a kind of poetry, he often claimed, but of a very different kind: an ugly, trustworthy poetry.

I could only presume the clippings had blown out to sea with the rest of his possessions, scattered back across the realm in which they belonged: randomness, chaos.

In the afternoons I re-explored the town, trying to find some trace of the past, some ancient layer or deposit beneath this new city rebuilt of suburbs and supermarkets, shopping malls and overpasses. The shoebox houses on their stork-stilts had largely gone: stout, squat homes hugged the ground everywhere, built out of bricks that no amount of monsoonal huffing and puffing would bring down.

Each evening I visited the hospice ward again, but communication was impossible in the evenings, and I rarely stayed at his side more than half an hour. He slept too deeply, refusing even to acknowledge the touch of cup or spoon to his lips.

His doctor was of no help. Each time I rang his rooms I received the same answer: Nothing Could Be Done.

The end came simply, suddenly: I was woken on my sixth morning, in the larger small hours, by a voice on the phone announcing that he had 'gone'. Is it always as undramatic as this? Nothing seemed altered at the hospice: Keller lay in the same position; even looked much the same colour as when I'd left the night before. But somewhere inside that frail, papier-mâché body, some last border had been crossed, something had gone missing, finally.

I slipped my arm beneath his head—almost weightless, emptied of life and mind and thought—and kissed him.

And then signed some papers, and walked out of the hospice into the new, unfamiliar Darwin.

From the street a car horn sounded, and then another, pitched slightly higher: a minor third. A soft, temperate rain was falling—slow, blunt, wet pinpricks—and the air seemed cooler than any Wet season I had known. I knew no-one in this rebuilt town, but wanted someone—anyone—to know that a Great Man had died, whatever the crimes he felt he had committed.

Back at the hotel I rang home—Melbourne, STD—but Rosie was already at work. I rang my father's surgery in Adelaide, listened politely to his recorded message—measured, pedantic—then left a brief message after the bleep. I rang my mother's library—engaged.

I rang the local paper, and asked for the newsdesk. After listening politely the voice referred me to the Classifieds, Death Notices:

'We have obituaries prepared for notable figures, of course. But in this case . . .'

I leafed through the phone book, looking for old friends, familiar names. Papas, Lim, Mitchell . . . The search was pointless—dozens of entries were listed under each. I began to ring at random: telling anyone who would listen. I rang the local doctor who had cared for Keller, listened absurdly to *his* recorded message, and left my own—an obituary.

Someone had to know what had happened.

Finally the futility of it all overcame me, and I left the hotel again: walking the streets restlessly, on edge, wanting to grieve but not quite knowing *how* to.

A Thai restaurant in Smith Street provided some sort of comfort. A soup thick with ginger and hot chillis warmed my stomach, and also—the heat spreading to nearby tissues—seemed to cheer my heart. The smile of the waitress—shuffling with tiny stylised steps, incapacitated by some absurd traditional Asian garment—also warmed me, and for an instant I considered asking her what time she finished work . . .

Not for sex, of course. Or if for sex only as a replacement for the kinds of physical intimacy that I needed at that moment and that money couldn't buy: the cuddles of my daughter; Rosie's leg draped over mine as we watched TV, her hands resting on my shoulders at breakfast as she leant across me, reading the headlines . . .

In my hotel room, my stomach swollen, glowing, I dozed on and off through the afternoon. I guess I was trying to avoid the knowledge that grew slowly inside me: that I had reached the end of a deep, last hope. While Keller had lived—no matter how many years since our last consultation—he had been a safety net, offering a faint last hope, a genetic lifeline back to Liszt, Czerny, Leschetizky; there had always been the possibility of returning to his room at the *Swan*, and preparing myself for a last assault on the world of music.

Now I was faced with myself for the first time: Paul Crabbe, greying, dissatisfied, fast approaching mid-life, my backside stuck fast to a minor chair in a minor music school. Able to dupe my audiences at the odd concert, and even the critics— no, *especially* the critics—but never for one moment, even at my most unguarded, deluding myself.

In this sense Keller was bad for me, the worst possible teacher: revealing perfection to me, and at the same time snatching it away. Teaching a self-criticism that would never allow me to forget my limits.

And so I have wasted the years since Darwin sitting at the piano, pressing keys and hearing only notes emerge, obsessed by technique in a way that he would never have approved.

'Only the second-rate never make mistakes,' he once teased.

And again, another version: 'Only those capable of ugliness can be beautiful,' a phrase I had failed to understand, and thought nonsensical, at the time.

But a second-rate perfection is all I have any hope of attaining: technical perfection, not musical perfection. Therefore, better second-rate than third.

I still often think of it in athletic terms—and envy the athletes their clocked goals, their fixed, measurable achievements. If I could leap ten feet in the air or run the hundred in ten seconds flat—*that* would be achievement. It could be measured, quantified. No-one could argue, quibble . . .

Least of all myself.

As I rose from the bed, the sun broke below the heaving clouds: a rare, golden light drenching, saturating the town. Always these deft, elemental touches move me: light breaking through clouds, rain spattering on roofs, pink sunsets. As I gazed across the town I was overcome by nostalgia . . . and regret that I had not taken more notice, kept a better record of those beautiful years. Never again will time move as slowly as it did then, and never again would there be so much to be discovered, to be touched and tasted for the first time.

And now it was too late: once we begin to sense our childhoods, we are no longer children. And decisions have been made—by omission, neglect, inertia—that cannot be unmade.

A painting I once saw often comes to me: an image that sticks. A grey interior, with one small door, off-centre, slightly ajar. And through that crack, heartbreakingly unreachable: golden light, green grass, a child with a hoop, playing.

Nostalgia is always as simple, as stylised as that: a child's game, a single glowing memory. Soon I would be flying back to the South: to the woman and child that I loved, within the confines of a life that I hated. But for a time I sat there, at the mercy of my own memories, my throat congested, tears seeping; mourning a great man, yes, but also mourning for myself—for the times and possibilities that would never come again. The roast meat, the kisses. The music around the piano. The light that always seemed to shine behind my mother. My father, rushing through the door holding high his first plump-fleshed, red-furred rambutan . . .

And Keller, sitting on his balcony in a shaft of sun, the smudged elbows of his white coat resting on a month old copy of *DIE PRESSE*, the gold ring on the mysterious stump of his finger, his ear-finger, glinting off and on, catching the light, the schnapps bottle beside him.

'Guten tag, Paul. Have you finished the Mozart?'

'Half-finished, maestro.'

'Is water at fifty degrees half-boiling?'

Can I know that mine was a foolish, innocent world, a world of delusion and feeling and ridiculous dreams—a world of music—and still love it?

Endlessly, effortlessly.

About the author

2 Meet the author

4 Life at a glance

About the book

6 The critical eye

8 Behind the scenes

10 The inspiration

Ideas,
interviews
& features
included
in a new
section…

Read on

12 Have you read?

16 Find out more

Meet the author

PETER GOLDSWORTHY was born in Minlaton on South Australia's Yorke Peninsula in 1951. He grew up in various South Australian country towns but, like the character of Paul in *Maestro*, moved to Darwin for his final years of high school. He studied medicine at the University of Adelaide and graduated in 1974. He is married with three children — one of whom, Anna, is a well-known concert pianist whose teacher Eleanora Sivan provided part of the inspiration for *Maestro*'s Herr Keller.

Goldsworthy works part-time in general practice in Adelaide, and spends the rest of his time writing. He describes the reaction to his dual careers: 'People often ask how I manage to mix working as a writer with working as a doctor. Or — an interesting wording — which are you "really"? I suspect that my temperament is more suited to writing than to medicine. Ever since I treated a fractured right leg in my first year out of medical school by putting a plaster on the left leg I've had a feeling that life held out something else for me beyond medicine. Fortunately no harm was done, except to my ego. I removed the still-wet plaster red-faced, and reapplied it to the other side. Creative medicine? Or gross negligence? I blame a wandering mind, a mind too often occupied elsewhere. I like to jot down ideas between patients in a notebook I keep for that purpose. Recently a chemist around the corner returned a prescription to me with the note that while he enjoyed the poem, he didn't think it one of my best.'

It's rare for a writer to win major awards across many genres — poetry, short stories, novels and librettos. Goldsworthy has published several collections of poetry, six collections of short fiction and seven novels. He has also written librettos for the opera of Ray Lawler's play *Summer of the Seventeenth Doll*, and for the award-winning opera *Batavia*, both with the composer Richard Mills. His acclaimed poetry has been set to music by leading Australian composers including Graeme Koehne, Richard Mills and Matthew Hindson. His novels *Wish* and *Honk If You Are Jesus* are currently being adapted for the stage; *Honk* and *Maestro* are being adapted for the screen.

Many of Goldsworthy's poems, stories and novels are widely published in the English-speaking world and have been translated into several European and Asian languages. He has won many literary awards at national and international levels, including the Commonwealth Poetry Prize, the South Australian Bicentennial Award and an Australian Bicentennial Literary Award. A book-length study of his work, *The Ironic Eye*, by Andrew Riemer, was published in 1994. A noted 'performer' of his own work, Goldsworthy's readings are characterised by what critics have called 'a wicked sense of humour'.

Maestro is a set text on Year Twelve syllabuses in several States, and was chosen for the inaugural Australian 'One Book–One Town' project. ∎

> ❛ Recently a chemist around the corner returned a prescription to me with the note that while he enjoyed the poem, he didn't think it one of my best. ❜

Life at a glance

BORN

Minlaton, South Australia, in 1951

EDUCATED

Numerous country schools, then at Darwin High School and the University of Adelaide

CAREER

1974–present: practising physician in Adelaide
2001–2005: Chair of Literature Board of the Australia Council
2002–present: Chair of Libraries Board of South Australia

PREVIOUS WORKS

Poetry
Readings from Ecclesiastes 1982
This Goes With This 1988
This Goes With That: Selected Poems 1970–1990 1991
After the Ball 1992
If, Then 1996 (includes songs from *Summer of the Seventeenth Doll*)
New Selected Poems 2001

Short Fiction
Archipelagoes 1982
Zooing 1986
Bleak Rooms 1988
Little Deaths 1993
Navel Gazing: Essays, Half-truths and Mystery Flights 1998
The List of All Answers: Collected Stories 2004

Novels

Maestro 1989

Honk If You Are Jesus 1992

Jesus Wants Me For a Sunbeam 1999 (first
    published in *Little Deaths* 1993)

Magpie 1992 (with Brian Matthews)

Wish 1995

Keep It Simple, Stupid (KISS) 1996

Three Dog Night 2003

AWARDS AND HONOURS

1979 Western Australian Sesquicentenary
    Literary Competition, winner of the
    short story section for *Memoirs of a Small
    'm' Marxist*

1980 Premio Bancarella Literary Award,
    Italian Festival of Victoria, for *Before the
    Day Goes*

1982 Commonwealth Poetry Prize, Anne
    Elder Award for Poetry and South
    Australian Biennial Literary Award for
    Readings from Ecclesiastes

1988 Australian Bicentennial Grace Perry
    Award for Poetry for *This Goes With This*

1996 *Honk If You Are Jesus* selected as a *Times*
    Literary Supplement International Book
    of the Year

2002 Helpmann Awards for Best New
    Australian Work and Best Opera, and
    Green Room Award for Creative
    Achievement for *Batavia*

2003 FAW Christina Stead Award; short-listed
    for Miles Franklin Award, New South Wales
    State Literary Award for Fiction and Colin
    Roderick Award; and nominated for Dublin
    IMPAC Award for *Three Dog Night* ∎

The critical eye

PETER GOLDSWORTHY is 'excellent at catching the bitter underside of joking, colloquial speech', says the *Poetry Nation Review*. And nowhere is this more evident than in his classic 1989 novel *Maestro*. Acclaimed novelist Caryl Phillips saw the book as 'a profound exploration of European exile and Australian adolescence ... beautifully constructed, elegantly performed, deeply moving', while Helen Garner wrote in the *Sydney Review* that she 'enjoyed *Maestro* enormously. Besides its thoughtfulness and bright sensuality, it has a playful quality, a love of jest, which appealed to me very much.' 'Australian callowness and European high culture: this novel explores the heart of each ... It is trim and taut and put together with the unerring economy of a true craftsman. A powerful story', agreed Les Murray.

'A beautifully crafted novel dealing with the tragic gulf between talent and genius; between the real and the spurious', said C J Koch, and in the *Australian Book Review*, Gerard Windsor wrote about the 'necessary elusiveness of perfection, the unplumbed ocean beneath articulateness, the ambivalence of beauty — these are the revolving concerns of Peter Goldsworthy, and handled not just with irony, but with an effervescent, compassionate wit. He can't help being funny, but he's wise too.'

In his review in the *Age*, D J O'Hearn thought that 'those who have read Peter Goldsworthy's several books of short stories and two books of poetry will know him as a writer of sharp wit and distinctly Aussie humour — laconic, barbed, with a ready eye for the absurd. His first novel does not disappoint us in any of these respects … it is a lively and very readable novel and those who have not yet encountered Goldsworthy will take great delight in a writer who cares for his craft and works at it with such skill that it all appears effortless.' 'Goldsworthy's exploration of youthful innocence and arrogance confronted by the realities of evil, guilt and emotional suffering is unrelenting yet uplifting. My only disappointment is that *Maestro* is so short', agreed Giles Hugo in the Hobart *Mercury*. And Andrew Riemer wrote in the *Sydney Morning Herald* that '*Maestro* is a splendid achievement, a wise, deeply felt novel that continues to haunt well after one has finished it. It is distinguished by subtlety, by economy and by a quality often lacking in even the best of recent novels — an unerring quality of tone.'

In confirmation of *Maestro*'s status as a contemporary Australian classic, in 2003 the novel appeared at number twenty-two on the Australian Society of Authors' list of the top forty Australian books ever published, as selected by their members, primarily other Australian writers. ∎

> ❝ A beautifully crafted novel dealing with the tragic gulf between talent and genius ❞

Behind the scenes
Writing Maestro

'*MAESTRO* IS the third novel I wrote,' says Peter Goldsworthy. 'The first, which was also set in Darwin, was so bad that I sold the manuscript to a library …with instructions that no-one was ever to read it without my written consent. The second is still being written. It's about a mathematician, and has a lot of maths in it. It will never be published. It has its own wardrobe at home — it's in its thirtieth draft, and the drafts are all piled up in their wardrobe. I like to say it's the first novel in the history of literature which is taller than its author. It also weighs more than its author.'

In 1988 Peter had been invited to Brisbane for a six-week stint as a writer-in-residence. He had been working on his 'novel in the wardrobe' and 'the frustrations of trying to finish it finally overwhelmed me. As Keller advises Paul: "We must know when to move on. To search too long for perfection can also paralyse." The search for perfection with that book … had almost paralysed me. I was alone, missing my family. Each afternoon rain would fall, warm rain, and the air would fill with humid, subtropical scents … Sitting in my study in Brisbane, smelling the tropical rain, I was transported back to the Darwin which I hadn't seen for years. I remembered stepping off the plane at 2 a.m. in January 1967 — into a night thick with heat and rain. The first sentences of *Maestro* that I wrote were from that time and place, 1967, not from the actual story. I gave my first experience of Darwin to Paul Crabbe, largely as it happened.

'On one level *Maestro* is a celebration of Darwin — or an elegy for the Darwin of my childhood that has gone forever — and perhaps never existed anyway, except in the world of nostalgia. But of course we always invent and heighten the past through the processes of memory …

'I wrote the first draft of *Maestro* very quickly — in three weeks. And if Darwin wasn't — or isn't — like that, I don't want to be disabused of my precious memories. *Maestro* is a book I still like, which is rare, since there are several of my books that I now detest.'

Like Paul, Peter learned the piano as a teenager, and still has a great interest in music. 'Since the publication of *Maestro*', he says, 'people often ask me if I am still playing. If there is a piano nearby, people often ask me to play, or request their favourite Chopin. In fact I am the world's worst pianist, the black sheep of my family, who are all good musicians. I do share certain qualities with Paul: he is something of a smart-arse at times, and a bit full of himself at times. I think we often create characters to parody, and even exorcise, unwanted traits in ourselves. But if there is a part of me in Paul, there is a part of me in many of the characters of *Maestro*.' ∎

❝ *Maestro* is a book I still like, which is rare, since there are several of my books that I now detest. ❞

9

The inspiration
The Holocaust and Australia

'NEARLY 4000 applications have been received by the Commonwealth Government from German and Austrian Jews for admission to Australia as permanent settlers …The flood of enquiries has embarrassed the Government, which is concerned as [*sic*] the possible effects on employment in Australia of such large scale immigration if the applications are granted. The Government is also concerned at the possible effects of the admission of large groups of persons who are likely to settle in self-contained communities and not easily be assimilated into the general community …'
Daily Colonist (Canada), 10 February 1938.

As the Nazis rose to power in Germany and Austria in the early 1930s, Australia became recognised as a potential safe haven for Jews and others wishing to escape Nazi rule and persecution in Europe. But Australia's restrictive immigration policy, designed to limit non-British immigration, made it difficult for dispossessed Jews and other 'aliens' who did not have £500 for 'landing money' or relatives already in Australia to gain permission to enter the country. There has been much debate about the Government's motives for the restrictions: were they were a result of entrenched anti-Semitism, a reaction to public sentiment, or something more sinister?

In 1937, as the situation in Europe worsened, the Australian Government began to show an increased interest and the Australian Jewish Welfare Society was

6 proportional to population size only Israel accepted more Holocaust survivors than Australia 9

10

established to organise aid for Jewish refugees. Despite this, at the Evian Conference of 1938, held to address the refugee issue, Australia refused to increase immigration quotas.

Five months later, in November 1938, the night of destruction that was the *Kristallnacht* pogrom helped to convince the Australian Government to change its policy. It was announced that 15,000 refugees would be accepted over the next three years. By the outbreak of war in late 1939, more than 7000 Jewish refugees had arrived in Australia, and by 1945 Australia had accepted 8200 Jews escaping from Europe.

But what about those who survived the Holocaust in Europe, like the character of Herr Keller, Peter's music teacher in *Maestro*? Many saw Australia as a place of escape from the turmoil of Europe. In August 1945 a Close Relatives Reunion Scheme was created. Holocaust survivors with family already in Australia became eligible for immigration, but there was still a quota system and many missed out. Other survivors were accepted on the basis of their work skills. But despite low quotas, less than those of the War years, proportional to population size only Israel accepted more Holocaust survivors than Australia.

Despite the difficulties, approximately 15,000 survivors settled in Australia between 1945 and 1949. All up, around 35,000 prewar Jewish refugees and postwar Holocaust survivors had immigrated to Australia by 1961. ■

Have you read?

Honk If You Are Jesus
(Angus & Robertson, 1992)
At the age of forty-five, Dr Mara Fox, world
authority on *in vitro* fertilisation, is burnt out
and weary of the human race. Offered a
Chair in Reproductive Medicine at the new
Schultz Bible College on Queensland's Gold
Coast, she makes the move — only to find
herself entangled in a bizarre scientific
nightmare.
'*A wickedly funny mix of sci-fi, medical
marvel, satire and romance which adds to the
already towering reputation of Goldsworthy*'
— Terry Sweetman, Brisbane Courier-Mail
'*Goldsworthy has surpassed even the haunting
Maestro with this superbly crafted jewel of a
book. It is truly an extraordinary novel. Put it
on your must read list*' — Avi Lavau,
Who Weekly
'*Subtly symphonic ... Dazzlingly imaginative
... it wouldn't surprise me if this novel came to
share a place with books such as* The Loved
One *or* Brave New World' — Les Murray,
Sydney Review

Keep it Simple, Stupid (KISS)
(HarperCollins, 1996)
Paul 'Mack' McNeil has a reconstructed knee,
an unreconstructed life, and a taste for Baci
chocolates. Porn-and-prawn nights at the
Club, early morning milk runs, and day and
night marital disharmony are the raw
material from which he must reshape his life,
as he struggles towards a new perception of
himself and his world.
'*Goldsworthy's genius as a writer is that he
engages us in a whole range of emotions from
humour to farce to profound sadness ... simply*

brilliant and utterly engaging'
— Peter O'Connor, Melbourne Age
'One of Australia's greatest storytellers'
— Giles Hugo, Hobart Mercury

Navel Gazing: Essays, Half-truths and Mystery Flights (Penguin, 1998)

These occasional essays chart a course through the various genres of writing that Peter Goldsworthy has investigated: fiction, science fiction, poetry, opera and film. A loose, extended exploration of his key themes: death, humour, the limits of language, the relationship of biology to thought and culture, and the role and responsibilities of art. And first love also gets a look-in ...
'The overall result is a refreshing read that focuses on issues that any cultural observer (Australian or international) will recognise as currently relevant ... Clarity of expression, a street-wise erudition, immense learning, a wonderful sense of the absurd and a love of life's odd-spots combine to allow the reader to breeze through ... almost without knowing we are being educated' — Ian Irvine, OzLit

Jesus Wants Me For a Sunbeam (HarperCollins, 1999)

A moving tale of loss and the relationship between parents and child, first published in the collection *Little Deaths.*
'This is an extraordinary work that exemplifies all of Goldsworthy's talents ... Its finale is magnificent' — Matthew Condon, Overland
'A tour-de-force of control and compression ... One of the many fine things in this splendid novella is Goldsworthy's meticulous description' — Andrew Riemer, Sydney Morning Herald

> ❛ One of Australia's greatest storytellers ❜

Have you read? *(continued)*

New Selected Poems (Duffy and Snellgrove, 2001)
The best of Goldsworthy's earlier collections, from the ironies and laconicism of *Readings From Ecclesiastes* to the more rhythmic and verbally playful poems of *If, Then*, plus various new poems, and a selection of songs from the libretto for the opera *Batavia*.
'*Stylish chiselled poems*' — The Oxford Companion to Twentieth Century Poetry

Three Dog Night (Penguin, 2003)
Is it possible to be too happy? When Martin Blackman returns to Adelaide after ten years in London, he has never been happier. A shadow falls across that happiness when he introduces Lucy, his English wife, to his childhood friend Felix, and finds Felix changed beyond recognition.
'*A story of love and jealousy brought to a powerfully orchestrated climax in the vastness of the central Australian desert. Goldsworthy's most ambitious novel thus far, his most intricately crafted, and his best*' — J M Coetzee
'*An intense and brilliant novel about the fathomless human capacity for self-deception … The novel's powerful climax is a measure of its accomplishment. It moves towards a dramatic instant, around which swirl all the ambiguities teased out by the narrative. Goldsworthy's prose is so smooth, it is easy to underestimate how artful it is; he is in command of his material … A work of concentrated formal elegance that confirms Goldsworthy's status as one of Australia's best novelists*'
— James Ley, Sydney Morning Herald

❝ Goldsworthy's prose is so smooth, it is easy to underestimate how artful it is ❞

'A beautifully told story that defeats the reader's expectations at every turn … Three Dog Night is an outstanding Australian story. Its subject will resonate, and its power will make it a strong contender for literary awards. It will appeal to readers of literary fiction, but it is so well told that it should enjoy a wide audience' — Lachlan Jobbins, Australian Bookseller and Publisher

The List of All Answers: Collected Stories (Penguin, 2004)
Stories extracted from four of Goldsworthy's major works, including Little Deaths and Bleak Room, plus recent stories that have not appeared in book form previously.
'There are stories here of magnificent achievement' — Gail Jones, Australian Book Review
'It is remarkable that there is an evenness to the tone and voice of two decades' work … Goldsworthy has been writing sharp … short fiction for a long time. Goldsworthy will scythe to the marrow with a beautifully resonant and rhythmic sentence … in this collection, he confirms himself as a writer to stain the lips with' — Christopher Cyrill, Sydney Morning Herald
'Poised, polished, witty and self-aware … A skilfully orchestrated, finely controlled collection' — Katharine England, Sunday Mail ■

ON THE WEB

www.PeterGoldsworthy. com
The author's own website, with biographical information, reviews of his previous books and much more.

www.holocaust.com.au
A website dedicated to Australian memories of the Holocaust.

http://math.boisestate. edu/gas/
The Gilbert and Sullivan archive, devoted to the operas and other works of William S. Gilbert and Arthur S. Sullivan. Includes clip art, librettos, plot summaries, pictures of the original G&S stars, song scores, midi and mpeg audio files, and newsletter articles.

Find out more

SEE

Productions of the operas *Batavia* and *Summer of the Seventeenth Doll*, with librettos by Peter Goldsworthy.

READ

Chopin's *Nocturnes* and B-Flat Minor Scherzo

The music of Liszt

Czerny's Opus 599

Beethoven's G Minor Concerto

VISIT

Darwin, Northern Territory (www.ntholidays.com.au)

Immigration Museum, Melbourne — explores stories of people from all over the world who have migrated to Australia from the 1800s to the present day. ∎